*"God almighty," Guardino said.
"This place is like a damned slaughter
house."*

*"No, it's lots worse," I said.
"Butchers are merciful. Armour and
Swift don't let cattle and hogs suffer."*

**With Deepest
Gratitude For:**

*The interest and encouragement
from my breakfast buddies
Ron, Rick, Bill and Cork*

From Fans' Reviews

Enjoyed the style of the author, brings the events into focus just like being there. 5 star.

Good military history lesson. Very descriptive and also entertaining. Realistic description of the ugliness of war and how politics interfere with the boots on the ground.

This was one of those books you pick up and start reading and can't put down.

I will read anything this author writes.

The authenticity is evident throughout. The combat seems so real, you can smell the cordite. - Chris G

Great book! Really like the way the Author writes. Can't wait for his next book.

This is the best Historical fiction I have read about World War II in Germany. Hopefully the author will write more.

My hat is truly off to the author. This book is wonderful. From start to finish it is an absolute page turner. There are few novels that i have read to date that truly capture the comraderie amongst fighting men.

Not what I expected, I expected a good book and got an excellent one.

This book takes you into the daily lives of the Union Soldiers. It give gave me a perspective of the horrors of this war. It should be used by history teachers in today's schools

Payne has crafted a realistic and impressive novel that at times convinces the reader he's smelling gun smoke and hearing the thud of bullets.

Having read three other of Scott's war stories, WW2 and Korea, I came to this Civil War epic with high expectations. I was not disappointed.

One of the best books I have ever read. A must read for any and all interested in the Civil War. Thank You J. Scott Payne.

ISBN: 978-1-944815-45-5

www.ArgonPress.com

To End All Wars

--- A Novel of World War I ---

By J. Scott Payne

Cover Design by Deanna Compton

Published in the United States of America
By Argon Press

ARGON PRESS

The Author's American Soldier Series

The Orphan
A Novel of the American Revolution

A Corporal No More
A Novel of the Civil War

To End All Wars
A Novel of World War I

Brought To Battle
A Novel of World War II

The Green Hell
A Novel of the Army's Pacific Campaign

The Trail Through Hell
A Novel of the Army's Pacific Victories

Chosun
A Novel of the Korean War

Prologue

In autumn 1917, revolution takes Russia out of World War I, enabling Germany to send millions of seasoned troops to the Western Front in France.

The Kaiser's army, now outnumbering British and French forces, launches a series of massive offensives. The allied line bends nearly to the breaking point.

But America has declared war on Germany. The Yanks are coming.

Slowly.

At first, the Doughboys arrive in driblets – one 28,000-man division in a conflict waged among millions.

The American youngsters, our great-grandfathers, are combat novices. French, British and Aussie veterans train them. In a series of minor battles – Siecheprey, Belleau Wood, Cantigny – the Yanks still are amateurish. But they take to battle with a ferocity delighting their allies and chilling the German command.

 Further confrontations with the hardest teachers – German infantry – teach the Yanks their trade. A bemedaled German officer later writes that he never saw such inept troops learn so rapidly and so well.

In the brutal 1918 Meuse-Argonne offensive, Yanks sustain horrendous casualties, as do the British and the French.

But fighting at last under a unified command, the allies and the Doughboys overwhelm the Second Reich in six weeks,

 ending a 4-year conflagration.

This is the story of a soldier in Blackjack Pershing's favorite regiment and how its troops became combat experts.

Chapter 1

Coblenz, Germany – December 1919

When some kid in my company gripes I bark at him.

He doesn't know how good he's got it. Not 'til he spends a night alone freezing his nuts off in the slop of a shell hole.

It was my longest, loudest, coldest night – flares floating down from an inky sky, artillery blasting holes in the muck around me, machineguns stammering. Despite the racket, I'd doze and my face would sag to that goo, startling me awake.

My shell hole, stinking of cordite and rotting flesh, was maybe thirty feet wide and three-fourths full of tan water. The hole wasn't circular, though. The shell that blasted the adjoining crater blew away the north side of mine, creating a figure eight mud hole with matching pond.

The ground was a fetid morass. Curl into a ball and you start sinking into the muck. So I had to lie spread-eagled, legs in the water.

Honest to God, these brats here in Coblenz get to sleep in *beds* and in houses. German host families may be somewhat surly about it, but they sure aren't shooting.

Stationed here with the Army of Occupation is about the softest duty I can imagine. But, like I said, the kids grouse. They're pissed off, for example, because General Allen restricted beer-buying between 1100 and 1400 and between 1700 and 1900. Meanwhile he hinted that we'd be smart to drill the kids or run live fire exercises outside town during those hours.

My God, how easy 1919 is.

In my shell hole that night last June, I was trapped 100 yards from our trenches. I wanted to dash to safety but didn't like my chances. Hun and Yank machineguns were cross-firing bursts right over my head, keeping me flat.

Archie Blackwell lay five feet away face-down in the muck, most of his body in the water. He hadn't made a sound for hours. As far as I knew, he and I were the remnants of our failed raid, and now he didn't count.

Major Creek ordered the trench raid. He said battalion headquarters wanted prisoners to find out whether our opposite numbers were fresh arrivals from Russia.

At dark, I led us snaking through the swampy holes and past the hummocks of no-man's land. We arrived at their lines okay. I busted a Fritz with my brass knucks. Knocked him cold. When Blackwell and I dragged him from his trench he came to and started struggling. No problem. Wrestling hogs in Chicago's stock yards long ago gave me rock-hard arms, chest and back.

But then the Huns counterattacked with machineguns and stick grenades. They killed our prisoner and who knows how many of my men. Hurling my grenades toward the Huns, I dragged Blackie, now leg-shot back across no man's land.

Machinegun fire trapped us just as we got to the crater. I cocked my .45 revolver in case any squarehead rushed us. None did. Blackwell said, "Jesus, Max! You laid me down here on some stinkin' body."

He raised up to move.

Thuk!

The slug knocked Blackie prone into the muck. I tilted him onto his side so he could breathe, but half his face was gone. So was he.

After vomiting into the pond, I let him settle back.

That was 1918 in France. Now, 1919 in a defeated Germany, my job is to just keep the troops sharp and in shape. I work hard at it because it keeps my mind off of last year.

By the way, Adamczak says the troops call me The Bark.

Chapter 2

Jefferson Barracks – December 1917

I'm Max Coleman, lieutenant, Company B, 16th Infantry Regiment, U.S. Army.

Never having even gone to high school, I'm not sure I qualify for so much rank. But that happens when an army balloons in six months from a hundred thousand men to almost four million.

I can't believe how easy Army training is now compared to the Old Army I joined. Nowadays, packed trains haul the kids here to camp by the thousands, same as the trains delivered cattle herds to the stock yards.

Back on the Fourth of July in 1909, Andy Hart and I bit on a recruiter's pitch. We ran into the guy, a lanky sergeant, after gawking at a rifle company in Chicago's Independence Day parade.

The troops looked sharp. Starched khakis, hard faces shaded under the old stiff-brimmed campaign hats. Officers carried swords. The troops held their gleaming rifles perfectly aligned. Hobnailed boots clacked the cobblestones in thrilling unison to a sergeant's chant -- *Yo lep! Yo lep! Lep rat lep!*

The recruiter stood us beers and carried on and all about how the Army issued summer *and* winter uniforms. He said that being big and lean, we already looked like soldiers. Said we'd get three squares a day, our own bunk with a clean straw mattress in a solid brick barracks.

It sounded lots better than drafty, flea-ridden flophouses out back o' the Yard.

"And no rent, men," he added with a toothy grin. "What's more, Uncle Sam *pays* you. Pay ain't a lot. But when y'all get free board and room, so what? And, fellas, they just issued us the newest rifle, the '03 Springfield! The pluperfect best. You can drive tacks with it."

At the time I didn't give a hog's ass about rifles. All I wanted was to get away from the stock yards where I worked since I was twelve.

See, in 1904 typhoid took my folks and Ellen, my sweet little sister. One week we was harvesting on our farm outside La Porte, Indiana. Next week we sickened. Three weeks later they buried Sis with my folks.

I recovered and the judge turned me over to a neighbor who bought our farm. I was to work for him 'til age eighteen when I'd receive money from the farm's sale.

The mean old bastard didn't give me five minutes to sorrow. He kept me away from school and my pals. He threw out my bedtime favorites *Treasure Island* and *Tom Sawyer* and hided me three times with a razor strop. I think he wanted to run me off so's to keep the money himself.

It worked.

With a bundle of clothes I sneaked aboard a west-bound Michigan Central freight. They kicked me off the train in Chicago. I wandered bewildered among indifferent mobs. Then a scrawny kid with a friendly grin said, "Hey, where you goin'?"

"I donno. Never been here 'afore."

"Wanna make some money?"

"You bet. I'm getting hungry."

"Well, come on, then. I'm Andy. Who're you?"

"Max. Max Coleman."

Andy walked me through an imposing stone gate with twin turrets and the carved head of Sherman the Bull. It was the Chicago Stock Yard. I joined Andy and the other boys who led the tours.

Nobody hired us, but the yard let us lead tours because it was good for business. For two bits, each of us guided a small party along the Yard's elevated boardwalks. Looking down, you saw everything.

Smelled it, too.

Ladies and girls held lavender handkerchiefs to their noses because the Yard was very, *verrry* ripe. Occasionally when Lake

Michigan's wind died, the stink was so thick you sorta had to shoulder through it.

Some girls wept in pity for the animals, but their eyes also widened in wonder. The Yard fascinated folk. Foreigners too. I once asked an English businessman if he ever met Robert Louis Stevenson. He snapped, "Bloody Scot radical! Dead and good riddance! Mind your sauce, boy. Just show me the processes."

They came from all over the world to see the processes. See, on a farm it took all day to butcher a steer. A Yard crew did it in under an hour. In fact, the Yard's processes fed, washed, killed, butchered, packaged, chilled and shipped hundreds of cattle a day. And hogs.

Andy taught me a lot. He showed how to speak to ladies on the tours as if they were their daughters' older sisters. That often netted me a smile and an extra penny or two.

Some girls were saddened. One asked, "The animals seem so melancholy. Do they apprehend what lies in store for them?"

"It wouldn't surprise me, Miss, what with all the noise … especially from them hogs." In her sorrow, she actually leaned against me. I patted her shoulder, causing her father to explode in fury. Had I been older and smarter I'd have snuck a kiss.

But then -- I forget -- either Armour or Swift hired several puffed-up dandies to guide the tours. Uniformed, they were, and too fancy for the likes of us. It forced Andy and me and the other boys to find real work down in the yard itself.

I was agile and strong enough to become a snatcher. My job was to hook a hog's back leg to a conveyor. The conveyor yanked the critters upside down wiggling and squealing to beat hell until the Sticker sliced their throats.

But let that go.

By 1909 Andy and I were tough. God gave me broad steeled fists, a big help those times we had to fight punks drifting around our digs back o' the Yard. Yet when we signed up we found Army training pretty demanding … much tougher than nowadays.

Today a sergeant can inflict only so much misery upon fifty recruits, a full platoon. Back when we joined, our training NCO at Jefferson Barracks outside St. Louis had only ten of us to abuse, barely a squad.

Yeah, the Army fed us decent – crackers, beans, spuds and mulligan. Eggs and flapjacks Sundays. But, boy, we worked for it.

On our first day Corporal McKinnis shouted, "First job, you whoresons, is to haul them ashes out'n the barrack furnaces and boilers! Dump 'em, and report to me in fifteen minutes all cleaned up! Then we're off to the mess hall so's you can peel the mess sergeant's potatoes!"

McKinnis was a pot-bellied oaf who constantly shouted and cussed at us.

"I don't know why I'm trying this," he yelled, once we finished the spuds. "You worthless sickly-looking bastards can't never measure up to my outfit. But, shit! Orders is orders. I'll make you soldiers or work your ruin."

He had us run around the parade ground four times. When we stopped in front of him gasping and sweating, he sneered. "Useless panty-wastes! Tomorrow you'll run my parade ground *six* times even if I have to kick your asses the whole way. You'll curse the whores who gave birth to you."

That comment made me boil. He had no call to bring mom into it. Even after five years, memories of my family remained precious -- especially mom, who taught strict but kindly in our one-room school.

Anyhow, pure, blind hatred made me determined to show the corporal I could outdo any damn thing he demanded.

First he trained us to Stand At Ease and how to assume the Position Of Attention. "Heels together, dipshit! Toes four inches apart! Thumbs along the seams of your trousers … pants, you dumb bastard!"

He locked us at Attention and At Ease so many times I felt like some stock yard machine. After several hours in new Army brogans, our feet burned like they were on red hot coals.

His swagger stick, though, helped us ignore burning feet. He smacked us with the stick to correct us -- bruising whacks at elbow or shoulder. Your stomach jutted out? He jabbed it hard, point first. He slapped your chin to make sure you pulled it in and then whacked your butt just to show he could. He slashed his stick across the right shins of kids who didn't know right from left.

Later, he and the stick helped us memorize names of famous Jefferson Barracks officers – Stuart, Johnston, Wheeler, Longstreet and the sainted Robert E. Lee. As an afterthought -- most drill instructors were southerners -- he mentioned Grant and Sheridan. Not a word about Sherman.

The corporal and his stick also taught us close order drill.

Drill isn't hard work, but St. Louis summers are humid and hot as hell with no Lake Michigan breeze. We sweated through those buttoned high-neck tunics with long sleeves, tightened cartridge belts and nine foot of puttee tight wrapped each ankle to knee,

Andy and I and two other recruits caught on quick. Even so, the corporal kept us at it -- "For'rard Harch! Lep flank…Harch! Column rat…Harch! To the rear…!" Maybe the city boys needed all the repetition because they didn't seem quite bright.

One night just before Taps I was trying to grasp the Scottish accents in *Kidnapped*, a novel from the post library. Reading helped me relax and avoid Kill Floor nightmares.

Andy murmured from the adjoining bunk that he feared nightmares about close order drill. "Max, if you hear me give marching commands during the night, wake me up! Okay?"

"Private Hart, if I hear marching commands from you, I'll kick your butt."

"Much obliged, Max."

Chapter 3

Jefferson Barracks -- 1909

One day after the corporal took us through the same drill routine a dozen times – and we performed it flawlessly a dozen times -- I made the mistake of telling him we had it down pat.

He rounded on me. "Think so, do you?" He slammed his fist right into my stomach.

Even with his taunting words and kicks, it took a while to get back to my feet, catch my breath and unclench my fists. A lieutenant walking past asked, "Corporal, wasn't that a bit drastic?"

"Sir, this here 'cruit learns real slow."

The lieutenant glanced at me. "Very well, corporal. Carry on."

"Sir!"

As my breathing resumed, the corporal snarled in my face, "Not one word, damn you! And don't the rest of you be giving me no hard looks, neither! I'll run all of you into the stockade for silent contempt. You think *I'm* tough? You'll do some real hard time there."

He turned back to me. "Now, you peawit, since you think you know all about close order drill, I'm assigning you a new drill.

"Double time your ass over to Supply and tell Sergeant Zuelke I said to issue you a shovel. You use that shovel to fill up his coal cart. Then you pull the cart to the mess hall and all four barracks and fill their coal bins.

"Asswipe, you got two hours to return Sergeant Zuelke's shovel and cart all clean and shiny. Then report back to me fresh scrubbed, cleaned up and ready for inspection."

Hate kept me going all though that backbreaking, sweaty, grimy afternoon … deepened it, if anything.

It also taught me to keep my yap shut.

# # #

The other thing that kept me going was that I could spend Saturday and Sunday afternoons at the post library. Mom had told me books helped us see the world's wonders. Her words meant nothing to me until I escaped the Stock Yard and was going through basic.

The librarian, who reminded me of Mom, urged me to try *Bullfinch's Mythology*. Its tales of Charlamagne and King Arthur immediately hooked me. I must have been a third of the way through it when I fell in love with my own Guinevere.

She was a golden-haired blue-eyed goddess sitting two tables away. I couldn't help staring and occasionally we made eye contact.

Fortunately, the librarian ordered me into her office.

"That young lady," she said, "is the post commander's granddaughter and you are a mere recruit and certainly no Lancelot. Moreover, young man, this is Jefferson Barracks, not Camelot. I give you good counsel, therefore, to keep your attention on your training. I very, *very* strongly recommend you refrain from use of our reading room and that you simply check out your books."

Over the next three months, I checked out *Bullfinch* seven times running. The librarian frowned and sighed at one point. "I ought not let you monopolize the book," she said. "But nobody else at the post seems to want it."

# # #

As I said, Lard Ass McKinnis taught me to keep my yap shut. I didn't even mutter when he started riding Johnny Ryan unmercifully.

Though a bit of a dimwit, Ryan could follow commands such as, "To the Rear…March!" To the manner born, he'd pivot with the rest of us and resume marching the opposite direction without missing a step.

But if McKinnis issued that same command, say, eight times in a row – as he often did – it paralyzed poor Ryan, causing the rest of us in the squad to fall all over him and each other. Then

McKinnis would laugh as he beat the bejaysus out of Ryan with his stick. After that would come an epic cussing for all of us.

We heard Ryan sobbing one night. The next morning he was gone. We figured he deserted. We had to forget it because, at last, they issued us firearms.

"Awww, bullshit," Andy said. "The Regulars get the new Springfields. All they give us trainees are these old Krag-Jorgesens."

We never did fire the Krags.

Corporal McKinnis and his swagger stick had us use the old rifles to master bayonet drill and the manual of arms. At first our arms ached from high and low jabs and blocks. But after two weeks of hefting the firearms and thrusting those wicked blades into imaginary Chinee Boxer rebels or Phillipino guerrillas, the rifles came to feel no heavier than pencils.

I'll never forget our first in-ranks rifle inspection.

Captain Benson was all rawhide and bone. Faded blue eyes set deep in a leathery face made him look about ninety. We nicknamed him snagglepuss. Anyway, First Sergeant O'Neill hulked two paces behind the skipper as they proceeded along our ranks.

The captain snatched the Krag from my hands. Giving off a strong whiskey odor, he snapped, "Repeat your First General order."

"Sir! My first General Order is to walk my post in a military manner, keeping always on the alert and observing everything that takes place within sight or hearing. *Sir!*"

He tossed the rifle back and ordered me to recite my chain of command. Being a reader, I knew it and rattled it off from Corporal McKinnis right on up to Chief of Staff General Bell, Secretary of War Taft, and President Roosevelt.

The skipper gave a ghost of a smile. "Very good, Private."

"Thank you, sir."

His wrinkles deepened in disgust and the first sergeant whacked my hat with his swagger stick. He bellowed "Damn you, Coleman! Enlisted people *never* thank officers! You just say, 'SIR!' and that is ALL! Is that *clear*, Private?"

"Yes, sergeant!"

That kind of sums up my first months at Jefferson Barracks, except for my few hours at the library.

I had to admit, though, that despite my hatred for Corporal McKinnis, military life surely beat sweeping hog blood off the Kill Floor. And the Mississippi River's odors were mild compared to the stock yard's solid reek.

The only really bad time for me was Christmas.

When I was a kiddy, Daddy would read *A Christmas Carol* to Momma, Ellen and me, trying to convert his Indiana twang to what he fancied was an English accent.

The living memories of those warm happy evenings helped ease the slave-like life of barracks and training.

Chapter 4
Jefferson Barracks -- 1909

Very late one Saturday night First Sergeant O'Neill and Sergeant Owens, a good egg, changed my life.

Just after midnight I was on guard duty when both NCOs lurched to the barracks, staggering drunk. Each supported the other as they climbed the concrete stair to the barracks door.

Though our NCOs frequently got soused, they usually were fairly quiet about it. This night, though, the two proclaimed their condition by singing – well, trying to sing -- at the top of their lungs.

O'Neill was a beefy giant with a squeaky little tenor. Owens, short and lean, had a pitch-perfect bull-frog bass just like old Mr. Perkins in La Porte's First Methodist choir.

Spreading his arms beneath the barracks porch light, O'Neill began an off-key version of *Going To The Animal Fair*.

> *All the birds and beasts was there,*
> *and the big baboon*
> *by the light of the moon*
> *was combing his auburn hair.*

Owens broke in, booming "The Monk, The Monk, The Monk" in a rumble so low and loud I swear it rattled the rafters.

But his timing was way off. O'Neill had yet to sing the lines about how the monkey sat on the elephant's trunk who sneezed and fell to his knees, killing The Monk, The Monk, the Monk etc.

Propping himself in the doorway, O'Neill told Owens, "Now Jim, dammit, we'll sing it again from the start. This time let's get it right! Wait for your proper time to join in."

I don't know if it was deliberate or just because he loved his own voice, but Owens again came booming in far too early, once more sabotaging O'Neill's solo.

O'Neill yelled, "Damn you to hell, Jimmy!" and took a roundhouse swing at Owens.

The smaller man ducked. Or, I don't know, maybe he passed out and collapsed.

Either way, O'Neill's ham-sized right fist missed Owens and struck the door jamb with a nasty crack.

Hissing in pain, the first sergeant bent over to cradle the injured mitt against his big gut. He yelled, "Damn your black soul, Owens, git up! Goddammit, I'm gonna knock you clean into next month."

It terrified me.

See, though on guard duty I was only a raw recruit. In accord with my First General Order, I sure was fully alert and observing everything in sight and hearing … including seeing my superiors brawl in public, a court-martial offense.

But General Orders said nothing about how a mere 'cruit should handle such a situation.

I stepped towards them, "Please, sergeants, can't we…"

I shut up when O'Neill turned, bleary eyes peering at me through his fog. Seeming to weigh my words, he twice nodded ponderously.

Then he swung at me.

Fortunately, his left hook was so slow it would draw flies. I ducked it, causing the first sergeant to lose balance. He fell past me into the darkened barrack, clattered against the platoon's rifle rack, and landed full length on the floor.

With considerable effort, Sergeant Owens managed to push himself upright. Leaning against the door jamb, he goggled at O'Neill. "Jesus, Coleman, you knocked old Pat out? Wished I seen that."

He giggled. "And all by yourself, too? You're sure big enough. Remind me never to fight you."

"Sergeant, I didn't touch him. Honest. I swear. I just…"

Owens held up a cautionary finger and said, "Shhhhhhh!" bathing me in beer fumes. "Serves the old son of a bitch right, trying to clout me that way."

Several half-awake men padded barefoot from their bunks to see what happened. They focused on O'Neill, flat on his back now snoring thunderously.

Owens shushed me again. "Not a word," he whispered. "Don't let it get out. You'd get a general court for striking a superior. They'd send you to Fort Leavenworth for life and one dark night."

"But…"

He held up the finger again. "Shhhhh!" The sound seemed to fascinate him.

Peering over the rifle rack, Andy Hart gave a creaky yawn and scratched his chest. "Max, what in hell happened to the first shirt?"

With a drawn-out belch, Owens took charge "Never mind what happened. You four! Carry the first sergeant to his room and put him on his bunk. Don't sling him around. Rest of you men, get back to your bunks and turn in."

"But sarge…."

"That's an order, Hart! This incident is closed. Go get some sleep."

The four men half-dragged O'Neill down the barrack's long center aisle.

Leaning close, Owens whispered, "Coleman, heed me now. Keep your mouth shut. Say nothin' to nobody. Everthang'll be all right."

He wobbled off in the general direction of his own room, booming, "The Monk! The Monk! The Monk!"

Chapter 5
Jefferson Barracks -- 1909

The next day, First Sergeant O'Neill emerged from sick bay with his right hand in a cast.

And I emerged from the barracks with a reputation.

The rumor was that with a single punch I knocked out O'Neill who had four ranks and fifty pounds on me.

My denials only received knowing smirks. Across from me at breakfast in the mess hall, Andy whispered, "Max, tell me true now. Did you really knock old O'Neill out?" From both his sides, McCarthy and Tomlin leaned in to hear me.

Swallowing a spoonful of beans I said, "Hell no, Andy. Never touched him. The man was falling down drunk."

He stared at me. I stared back and bit into my cornbread. Andy nodded and grinned, "Yeah, Max. Sure. Okay. Your secret's safe with me." Tomlin grinned, too. McCarthy snorted in derision.

When we assembled for drill, Corporal McKinnis gave me several uneasy sidelong looks. In turn, I gave him a mean smile.

He never again touched me with his goddamned swagger stick.

During drill that morning, Sergeant Owens walked past us and caught my eye. He held his finger alongside his nose and said "Shhhhh" again.

I worried about what the first sergeant might do. But as far as I know, he never said a word about the incident. I guess he either was a black-out drunk or never heard the rumors.

# # #

The following month, McKinnis released half of us from recruit training.

"You younkers done okay," he said. "You sure ain't ready to fight Moros or the Hucks in the Phillipinoons, but maybe you'll catch on.

"From here on you report to Company B, onliest infantry here at the Barracks. I hear they's building up for work along the Mexican border.

"I also hear the company commander loves hiking so you'll get some blisters on your dogs. But first, Sergeant Owens gets his mitts on you. He'll teach you all about the '03 Springfield."

Owens issued us the sleek new rifles. He showed how to remove the bolts so we could clean the cosmoline from the actions. He also ordered each of us to memorize his rifle's serial number.

All we did next day, however, was sling the rifles on the shoulder opposite our blanket rolls and set off with Company B on our first twenty-mile hike. Halfway through the day, Hart shook the dust from his bandanna and said, "I thought we'd done a lot of marching during drill. But this here captain is rough on rats. We damn near been running."

The rest of us snuck a sip from our canteens, mopped our sweat and saved our breath.

Only two of us -- Charlie Lloyd and Fred Ulrich – straggled during the march. They both wheezed and seemed to have lung problems.

That evening back at our bunks, we just sat kind of numb for a spell. Andy pulled at his left shoe which came off with a sucking noise. "Damn that hurts! I think I've been walking on more water than the good Lord hisself."

"Yeah," I said pulling off my right sock. "Look at this blister on the ball of my foot. Big as a silver dollar."

"How would you know, Max? Never seen anything bigger than a dime in your whole life."

I was too tired for even a weak chuckle.

We were hobbling the next morning when Sergeant Owens arrived. "Okay, men, once each of you correctly recites your rifle's serial number, we'll learn you all about these pieces."

In the boredom of yesterday's forced march, I constantly recited 2763566 to myself. So, unlike the other men, I had no problem.

Owens forced the others to stand at ramrod attention, hold their rifles in front of their faces and read the serial numbers aloud until they could do it from memory.

It only took about fifteen arm-quivering minutes. "See, men," he said. "It's easy. Just takes some effort."

For a sergeant, Owens was surprisingly quiet and patient, joking more often than cussing. In that way he reminded me of Dad who was strict and demanding, but kindly and relaxed.

Owens sat us at a long table, our rifles before us.

"Men, now you're going to learn about the U.S. Rifle, Model of 1903, also called the Ought Three Springfield. Unlike that Krag you trained with, this rifle's bolt has twin locking lugs and a strong heat-treated receiver. That means it can fire a much more powerful round.

"Your '03 has a maximum effective range of a thousand yards and, if you aim right, you can hit targets at seven hundred yards. She is your sweetheart and your first love. Treat her nice, men, care for her well and she'll save your life."

He held up a gleaming brass cartridge. "Here's what we feed her -- the Catridge, ball, caliber .30, Model of 1906. We call it Thirty Ought Six for short, *never, ever* to be confused with that weakling Thirty-Thirty.

"Men, don't ever ask me why they call this here pointed spitzer bullet a ball. That's just how the army does it and that's all you need to know."

Continuing to keep my yap shut, I refrained from asking why he called it a "catridge" rather than "cartridge" as it was spelled. Same reason they called it a ball, I guess. Just because.

"Now the first thing we learn," the sergeant said, "is how to break down the bolt so's you can clean it and protect it from corrosion. We start here at the bolt's ass end with the safety lock and the cocking piece."

It took him half a dexterous minute to reduce the bolt to its dozen parts.

"An important warning, boys! Heed me, now. I mean it!

"Notice that when I disengaged the striker from the firing pin spring and firing pin sleeve, I pointed the whole assembly well away from my mug. Otherwise the compressed spring could spear that striker into an important piece of govmint property -- your eye.

"But even if it misses your face, that spring still could throw the tiny little striker twenty foot away into the brush or mud. If you can't find it, the Army issues you a new one and deducts four bucks from your pay."

We spent all day disassembling and reassembling the '03, memorizing its nomenclature from the fore end sling swivel to the bayonet stud and from the extractor collar and to the butt plate latch.

The next morning, the sergeant warned us to moisten little rolls of cloth or paper for ear plugs. On sore blistered feet, we hobbled to the range. Once we arrived on the firing line, we set our rifles on the rests and hunkered down beside them. The sergeant issued each of us one cartridge.

"Lock and load one round of ball ammunition!"

"Ready on the Right? Ready on the left? Ready on the firing line!

"Fire!"

That first shot was a hell of a shock – like being clouted or taking a body block in the shoulder.

Striding back and forth before us, Owens said, "Kicks, don't she?"

We all nodded, wide-eyed.

"Actually," he said, "there's no kick at all.

"What happens is called muzzle jump," he said. "When that bullet exits the rifle bore, the barrel is propelled upward in a short arc based on the rifle's center of gravity. It only seems like a kick because of that loud report."

That's bull. It's a kick, a stout one. But by then all of us had enough muscle padding to handle it.

Sergeant Owens first directed our focus at the 25-yard sighting targets.

Excited to hit the mark, we soon became accustomed to the rifles' noise and kick. By the time we got the sights zeroed, I felt as if my '03 and I were one thing. The recoil's effect seemed to be no more than a gentle unconscious backwards rock.

When we started firing at three hundred yards most of the guys had a hard time hitting the target, let alone its bullseye. But either I had better eyes or a better rifle, or both. I had no difficulty punching holes in the bull.

"Okay, buster," Sergeant Owens said. "Let's see how you can do at six hundred. Prone position."

At six hundred yards I managed to punch a saucer-sized trefoil of holes in the bullseye. He had me try the same target from my favorite position, seated with elbows on knees. Same result.

Owen whistled. "Jesus, Private Coleman, if you can keep that up you'll qualify as an expert – that pays an eight buck bonus each month. We'll bring the range officer out here tomorrow and see if you can do it again."

I won in a walk and smirked to myself.

Hart and Private Joe Davies finished a long ways behind me.

Chapter 6
Jefferson Barracks -- 1910

Some weeks after recruit training ended and we joined B Company, Corporal McKinnis stepped on his crank.

He returned to the barracks drunk one night and picked a fight with somebody.

"What I hear," Andy told me, "is that the MPs had to break it up. They arrested both men and hauled them to the stockade. This morning, the CO busted McKinnis to private, confined him to post for a month and fined him ten bucks."

"Is this for real?"

"Max, it's Gospel truth. I got it from Bill Simpkins who was last night's CQ."

"Well, that's about the best damned news I've heard since joining the army. Dirty bastard!"

The news got even better.

Late that afternoon, a runner gave me orders to report to the company commander. When I arrived at the orderly room the duty NCO told me to report to Lieutenant Creek.

"I thought I was to see Cap'n Benson."

"Nope. The cap'n went tits up last week. Too much whiskey for too many years. First Lieutenant Creek is the skipper now. He's a good man. Now go knock on his door."

I rapped on the door with the frosted glass. The lieutenant said, "Come!"

I did, snapping to rigid attention. "Sir, Private Max Coleman reporting as ordered."

"Coleman," he said, "I heard you're good with your fists so maybe you can handle the men."

"Sir?"

"I'm picking you to be your squad's lance corporal."

I couldn't believe it. The Old Army didn't promote you during your first hitch. Not ever.

"Well?" he said.

"Sir! I'll do my best!" I gave him a blistering salute.

He grinned. "No 'Thank you'?"

"Sorry, Sir, I was ordered never to thank an officer."

"Corporal," he laughed, "that was in the olllllld army. Now you can speak to officers. Thank 'em, even." He waved me out of the office.

It turned out that lance corporal isn't an advancement in rank but an appointment. My pay remained $15 a month though at least my single stripe got me off spud peeling if not KP. It probably was a test whether I could get men to obey me.

The next night I ordered Private Flannery to straighten the contents of his foot locker per regulations – socks neatly rolled, underwear square folded, shaving mug, brush and safety razor in the center.

Flannery jeered, "That lousy stripe don't make you my boss, Coleman. So just go shove it up your butt!"

I was ready to invite him out behind the barracks when Hart tugged the Irishman's sleeve and whispered to him. Flannery glanced at me. I heard him whisper back, "No shit? He cold-cocked O'Neill?"

"One punch," Hart said. "Guys on first floor seen it."

Flannery gave me a wide smile. "Okay, boss," he said, and immediately went to work on his locker.

# # #

My promotion to actual corporal took some maneuvering plus fifty bucks.

Sergeant Owens explained it to me.

"Look, Max, being's how you've turned out to be a hell of a marksman, the officers want you to help train the men on the rifle range. But first you got to be an NCO."

"Well, I can't be an NCO until I'm in my second hitch, right?"

"Right."

"So I'm sunk. I've got just over two years left to serve in my first hitch."

"Now, lance corporal, there's more'n one way to skin a cat. What you have to do is buy out of this enlistment and reenlist in a different outfit."

"Buy out? What do you mean?" It was news to me that the Army let people buy out of the service. It wasn't the sort of detail the Army gives recruits. Not that it seemed to matter. I didn't have anything like the fifty dollar fee.

"Sarge, I guess I could hitch a railroad trip back to the old farm. I'd kick that old bastard's ass, squeeze the money from him and be back here in a week."

Sergeant Owens shook his head. "Lance Corporal, it might feel good to beat him up, but the local sheriff would nab you and turn you over to the MPs. That's a fast ticket to Fort Leavenworth. For soldiers to beat up on civilians – even mean old skinflints – breaks every law in the books.

"You'd best think up something else."

Hart came up with suggestion to buy a pair of clippers and go into business as a battalion barber for a nickel a throw.

It took almost three months to pay off the loan to buy the clippers and to amass $50. At first, squeezing those clipper handles for as few as ten minutes gave me a hell of a cramp in my hand. But I persevered. It also took a while to master giving a decent haircut.

The high point came late the third month when Lieutenant Schimmelpfennig brought his small twin sons to me. As I sheared away their curls they wailed, of course. But their dad seemed to enjoy the show.

He not only paid me twenty cents, twice my rate, but kicked in a nickel tip. "Thanks," he said. 'Now my sons look like boys instead of girls."

# # #

So, for 50 bucks I "retired" from the Army.

Then I reenlisted to join Company A, the dragoons. By prearrangement, the captain of A Company then permitted me to transfer back to Lieutenant Creek's B Company.

It now being my second hitch, the lieutenant promoted me to corporal and assigned me to help his riflemen improve their marksmanship.

It made me rich. As a corporal, my pay rose to $18 a month. Once Finance Corps finally processed the paperwork, I also received an $8 marksmanship bonus each month.

Once I started as a training NCO, Private McKinnis gave me a lot of dirty looks. I had words with him. "Look, McKinnis, if you got a problem with me, we can step out behind the barracks. I'll find out how far I can sink my fist into your blubber. Otherwise, knock it off. Clear?"

"Yes."

"Yes, what?"

"Yes, corporal."

I bequeathed the clippers to Private Sam Wilson, a squad mate. He needed to pay off his cigarette debt at the post exchange.

See, most of us used Bull Durham to roll our cigarettes. It only cost a nickel a pouch, enough to last a week. Hell, many company grade officers used Bull Durham and I've even seen a major or two roll their own.

But Wilson's taste ran to factory-made Pall Mall smokes which cost a quarter a pack. He smoked almost pack a day, leaving him less than nine bucks of his pay for other expenses.

So, as we put it back then, Wilson lived on jawbone.

He ran an account at the PX and borrowed from A to pay on the account. Meanwhile he promised A he'd get the money from B hoping C might forget yet another loan to buy beer.

During his first month as a barber, Wilson gave a hell of a lot of free haircuts.

Chapter 7

Jefferson Barracks -- 1910

To help new soldiers improve their rifle marksmanship, I borrowed heavily from Sergeant Owens' teaching methods.

"Don't shout at men who shoot bad," Owens said. "It only gives them nerves. Makes 'em shoot even worse. You got to be patient.

"I find that it helps," he said, "if you lay yourself right down beside a prone shooter and watch his face and hands as he fires.

"They usually flinch. He just shuts his eyes, you know, jerks at the trigger and that damn bullet winds up somewhere near Kansas City."

The problem was to get shooters to relax, which is where Owens' favorite training story helped.

"Now, boys, let's say on some dark night you're out on a country lane in the buggy with some beautiful girl. Old Dobbin is pulling you along real quiet-like."

His voice sank almost to a whisper. "Jest a quiet clip-clop, clip-clop, you know? So you and this girl kiss and finally she lets you unlace her bodice. You explore them alabaster bosoms. And when your mouth first touches one of them sweet, tender little nipples..."

Now he shouted.

"So, do you squeeze it or do you bite it?"

"You squeeze it, Sarge!"

"Damn straight! You squeeze it! You got to do the same with Miss Springfield. When you're on the firing line, just picture her in your mind. You just got to *squeeeeeze* that trigger.

"Boys, she'll reward your tenderness and give you full satisfaction."

Sergeant Owens, Sergeant Johnson and I told the story so many times we went blue in the face, but it seemed to help.

Most of our boys got so they routinely hit bullseyes at four hundred yards – pretty fair shooting -- and some as far out as six hundred.

As new recruits wound up basic training and rotated to the company, we introduced them to Miss Springfield, teaching them to treat her tenderly.

The day came when Lieutenant Creek told us the company was close to its full roster, one hundred seventy men and officers. "First time since the war with Spain," he said.

When that war ended in '98, Lieutenant Creek commanded a platoon. Now, twelve years later commanding four times as many men, he still was a lieutenant.

It made me curious. But it seemed smarter to ask Sergeant Owens rather than the lieutenant why our CO still wore only a single silver bar.

"Congress just keeps on cutting the Army's funds," Owens explained. "They want a small Army to guard the Indians and to keep the Mexicans out. Because Congress is such a bunch of skinflints, the army only has so much money for captains.

"Our CO has been a looie since graduating from West Point in '97. He was a second lieutenant then. Now he's a first. I heard him joke that maybe if a dozen or so colonels and majors die of old age, the Army may promote him to captain …if he ain't already died of old age.

"Meanwhile, get your squad ready to pack up," Owens added. "The word is we're moving to Texas because the Mexicans got themselves some kind of a revolution going."

# # #

"Hey corporal," Private Davies told me, "that black hair of yourn looks like it went and turned tan during the night."

I sat up from my bunk and flapped my blanket, producing a dust cloud.

"Yeah," I said, brushing at my gritty scalp. Wind got up last night so now everything's dusty. The Rio Grande is a hundred yards away, but Camp Cotton is a damned desert."

Camp Cotton and El Paso nestle by the big bend where the Rio Grande turns southeast to take over from the New Mexico state line as the American-Mexican border.

We're east of town next to a rail spur and the stock yard's holding pens.

Maybe the camp got the name because we moved into six-man tents by now sun-bleached cotton white. No more comfortable multi-story barracks with screened windows for us, no sir.

Oh, but breeze? We had plenty of that with the tent aprons rolled up. Roll 'em down and you swelter. Roll 'em up and you stay a bit cooler and eat dust.

"Say, Max, remember that recruiter fella back in Chicago?"

"Who, Andy? You mean the one promised us comfortable barracks?"

"Yeah, that's the one. The bastard lied to us."

"Naaa, he didn't lie, Andy. He just didn't bother to tell us the govmint always finds the worst conditions for soldiers to live in. So instead of just mosquitoes and heat along the Mississippi River, now we got mosquitos, worse heat, black flies, scorpions, rattlesnakes and cactus along the Rio Grande."

"Don't forget the dust."

"We won't."

Remember me complaining how hot it was in summer at Jefferson Barracks?

Well, summer in eastern Missouri is nothing compared to a sunny July day at Camp Cotton in southwest Texas. By mid-morning the heat itself feels solid. It just weighs on you. The sun actually stings your bare skin even after you get tanned. Takes some getting used to. And you have to drink water constantly.

The Army put us aboard the Missouri Pacific to El Paso so we could help keep the peace along the Mexican-American border. But it never was quite clear how we should do that.

"Sergeant Owens, what do we do to keep the peace here in Texas? Do we just shoot all the trouble-makers?"

"The trouble-makers, Max? Let's see. Which trouble-makers do you mean? American bandits? Or maybe you're talking about Mexican bandits? How about gun-runners? Or revolutionaries? What about cattle rustlers on both sides of the border?"

"Hell, half the Americans living in El Paso are of Mexican descent. They lived in El Paso for generations before it became part of America. Others just crossed the bridge from Juarez a week ago. So how do you tell the difference?"

"You can always turn your back, Sarge."

Supposedly, we were a select unit, trained as skirmishers because we all were good shots.

Sergeant Owens drilled it into our brains.

"Skirmishers are to advance upon the enemy in a wide line, keeping three to five yards' separation. Once given the order, you fire independently, picking your own targets."

Lieutenant Creek buttressed that concept. "That's how we succeeded in Cuba," he told us. "The dagos with their Mauser rifles chopped up our first close-order attacks on San Juan Hill.

"But we learned. Keep your spread and you're less likely to get shot. And when somebody shoots at you, you duck and stay low and fire from behind cover."

He said old officers and NCOs from out west, veterans of the Indian wars, would understand.

It happened, though, that some new officers at Camp Cotton confused things. They spoke of the need for troops to stand tall shoulder to shoulder and to proceed forward in nice straight lines firing in controlled volleys.

Overhearing such conversations, I asked, "Sarge, what's going on? That isn't the way we're supposed to deploy."

"Max, do you remember me saying 'Shhhhhh'?"

"Sure."

"Okay. Shut your hole!"

"But you trained us…."

"Corporal, you're thinking again. Ain't I warned you about that? Officers think. Officers give orders. We soldiers follow orders. That's it."

"Well, damn it…"

"Just let it go for now," he said. "With time they'll probably catch on."

Some never seemed to.

Chapter 8

El Paso -- 1911

One thing was sure. In Texas, we found few enemy to advance upon either in closed or open order. We just mainly hiked.

In either squads or platoons we patrolled along the Rio Grande's big bend, south and east of town. We also hiked up McKellan Canyon into the Franklin Mountains north of town. Sometimes we hiked west across the bridge into New Mexico where the border was just a single strand barbed-wire fence.

All the trails were dusty hot, but at least we sometimes got to take a break in the shade from the tall cottonwoods and willows on the Rio Grande's banks, or from outcroppings in the canyon.

Just like during the Indian wars, we left detachments at ranches or small towns along the border. Once my squad and Second Lieutenant Dickerson spent two weeks at Columbus, New Mexico, just off the border with Mexico.

It was a big, big change from Jefferson Barracks, and not just the weather. "Hoo, boys! Would look at all them redskins a-comin' down the trail at us?"

The red skin in question belonged not to Indians but to our sunburned faces. Remarking from horseback, hands folded on the blanket at his saddle's front, was First Sergeant Alexander Hamilton Willis.

Favoring us with a relaxed wide grin, Willis otherwise looked ready for action. He carried a pistol, a saber at his belt and a Krag carbine in his saddle holster.

What first caught our attention, though, was that he was a Negro. He belonged to the one troop of the 9th Cavalry which returned to El Paso last year from the Philippine Islands.

Willis not only was a veteran of the Indian wars but also battles in Cuba and three years of fighting Moros in the Philippine Islands. I'd say he was in his sixties because his beard was frosted with white. But he looked hard as nails.

Sergeant Owens grinned up at him. "Don't worry, sarge. Won't be long afore we're as dark as you fellas. Now why don't you slide down off that poor frothy-mouthed nag and give her a rest?"

Willis said, "Get down from my Tess? Hell, no! My feet might get sore like yours." He turned Tess's head and steered his troop -- hooted with laughter -- to clip-clop past our left flank.

Owens chuckled. "Friendliest exchange I ever had with cavalry."

"Why's that?"

"Well, horse soldiers and foot soldiers mostly trade nothing but insults."

"How come, Sarge?"

"After you've done six or seven more twenty-miles hikes," Owens said, "it dawns on you that riding would be a lot easier. So most infantrymen are jealous of how good the cavalry has it.

"Of course," he added, "most infantrymen don't know that the cavalry spends a hell of a lot of time – morning and night – cleaning their animals and shoveling their shit.

"The horse soldiers have got to feed and water those beasts before they can so much as nibble their own rations. And sometimes it's too damned hot in these parts for the horses, so the riders often must walk, just like us, leading their animals.

"But here's the heart of the matter," he said. "You're better off as a foot soldier. You might wish you could ride. But when people start shooting at you, an infantryman can hit the dirt lots faster and flatter than somebody perched on a nag four or five feet in the air."

Some officers warned us not to fraternize with the so-called buffalo soldiers. "Watch out, men, 'cause niggers can be tricky. They're likely to gang up on white men, sometimes knifing or beating them to death."

The warnings didn't make much sense to me. I worked alongside Negros in the stock yard. Yeah, their color was different and some had strange accents – but no stranger than the paddies just off the boat. Mainly they just seemed like ordinary folk.

"I don't like them blackamoors *or* Mexicans," Davies told me. "Just got no use for somebody whose skin ain't white."

"Well, I don't know about Mexicans," I said, "but these Negro troops have white officers who seem in pretty good health. The buffalo soldiers sure ain't ganging up on them, are they?"

"I don't care," Davies said. "They ain't white."

"Funny thing about that," Hart said.

"What?"

"Those white cavalry officers look down on us whites 'cause we're infantry. What's more, I overheard one of their lieutenants brag to one of our officers about how tough those buffalo soldiers are. Said they fight like devils."

Sergeant Owens and I found that on an NCO level, we and members of the 9th Cav got along fine.

Having been in El Paso a while, 9th Cav troopers knew the area well. They tipped us off to which were the best whore houses. They also knew which Mexican families made the best tamales, chili and fajitas. Most important, they told us where and when we might surprise rustlers or revolutionaries…or be ambushed by them.

Seeing me hawking, spitting and coughing one day, Sergeant Willis recommended that I try sleeping at night with a dampened bandanna draped over my mouth and nose.

It took some getting used to, but after that I inhaled a lot less dust and suffered a lot less catarrh.

Chapter 9

El Paso -- 1911

Other than freezing in winter, baking in summer, eating dust all year and patrolling daily, we did very little during the next three years at Camp Cotton.

Personally, I moved beyond *Bullfinch's Mythologies*. Tales of argonauts and the golden fleece of chivalry and Charlamagne or didn't relate well to chasing bandits through Texas cactus and rocks.

El Paso had a nice little library and where there's a library you always find one of the most helpful people on earth – the librarians.

One problem. They couldn't find any U.S. Army military manuals. There didn't seem to be any. Ah, but they found a fine British military manual. I was reading *Hasty Fire Cover and Concealment* one night when somebody began shouting "Stand to! Stand to!"

It was First Sergeant O'Neill. "Full uniform, canteens and rifles. Draw ammo bandoleers from Supply. We might have a fight on our hands."

Before dawn Company B lined up along the north bank of the Rio Grande. We saw flashes and heard gunfire as a rebel force begin to assault Juarez, the Mexican city across the river. Though we had ammo, the officers ordered us not to load our weapons.

Far outnumbering us along the river bank were most of El Paso's townspeople who turned out to see the action. Some were betting about who'd win and the idea caught on.

By noon Andy announced, "I got two bucks that says the Juarez garrison wins.

"The revolutionistas might outnumber the garrison, but the soldiers got cannon and machineguns. They'll mow them rebels down like wheat."

"We'll see," Sergeant Owens mused. "I think Villa's gang could whip the garrison. Depends on how he goes about it. You notice his troops don't seem to charge headlong against all that firepower."

"Villa?"

"Yeah, Pancho Villa. He's the revolutionary who's been raising Caine all over Chihuahua for years. Him and some other fella."

"What's Chihuahua?"

I said, "Jesus, Simpkins, Chihuahua is one Mexico's states, just like Texas or Missouri. For God's sake, you been looking at it right across the river for three solid years now."

It was the first time most of us saw battle. It was a bit disappointing because the combatants did their best to stay out of sight. Suddenly, the dry text of *Hasty Fire Cover and Concealment* seemed very real to me.

I believe we witnessed the boldest tactic of the day. A squad-sized group of men sprinted along the river's opposite bank to seize the Juarez end of the bridge to El Paso. Soon a second squad joined them and then a third.

"Ha!" Owens said. "Smart move! Now I bet they're closing the water intakes. The *federales* are going to get very thirsty"

"Those rebels got no uniforms," Flannery said. "They just wear any old work clothes.

"So what?" I said. "They all carry rifles. And they know how to use them."

We heard the pop-pop-pop of rifle fire. Machineguns rattled as fire fights built up and died out. Sudden fountains of dust and smoke sprang into view in the town as heavy blasts punctuated the small arms fire.

I asked, "Is that artillery?"

"Could be," Owens said. "But somehow it sounds different from those *federales'* cannon."

The battle became close and real when a cluster of wounded people hobbled across the bridge seeking aid. Two old men were trying to help three women and several children.

For the first time I got a look at the injuries bullets inflict.

One woman gasped with each limping step because a bullet or piece of shrapnel had gouged a furrow deep along her thigh. The arms of the other two women looked so shattered they seemed to have multiple elbows. Two children collapsed at the center of the bridge but three others were almost to our side of the river when citizens rushed to help.

Something had torn away one little girl's left cheek and some of her teeth. Her sister was using both hands to hold together a gaping stomach wound. The boy with them seemed uninjured. He was just staring.

"Jesus, now I wonder why I joined," I said.

Owens slapped me on the shoulder, "It's rough, Max. That's the nature of our trade."

"God help us."

# # #

Three days later the *federales* surrendered.

"Two things won the battle," Lieutenant Creek told us the next week in a meeting with NCOs.

"First, the rebels cut off the town's water supply. Then they blasted *federalista* positions with dynamite stolen from mining companies. That forced the army to keep contracting their lines until, as I hear tell, they were down to four or five adobe houses and no *agua* at all.

"So then it was a case of surrender or die of thirst and gangrene."

A few days later, the El Paso *Herald* said the battle was a big victory for the revolution, forcing President Diaz to flee Mexico. Yet the war went on. The victors fought each other, their battles sometimes spilling across the border that we patrolled constantly.

People on the American side of the line, even Mexican-born folk -- seemed to appreciate our presence. Folks on the other side hated us. Sometimes they threw rocks and, I guess, cursed at us. Sometimes they shot at us.

During those years around El Paso, our platoon engaged in perhaps a dozen skirmishes if you could even call them that. Quick little firefights at dusk or dawn with bandidos or revolutionaries – or maybe they were the same thing.

As I remember, we only had one injury that whole time. A lance corporal took a bullet in the rump. I don't think we ever caught or shot one of the bad guys.

"This is getting tiresome," Ulrich said. "We never catch sight of anything more than shapes ducking and fleeing through the willows."

"Yeah," I said, "but I think it has toughened us. We can handle desert heat now and nobody in our squad has a problem carrying two canteens, plus rifle, plus a hundred-round ammo bandoleer, plus camp gear."

Meanwhile the sun burned most of us as dark as our comrades on horseback.

# # #

Let's see, what else?

To make myself look older, I grew a moustache. Almost every NCO and most officers sported his own cookie duster.

Yeah, and I also fell in love in an odd way.

It started one evening when I bought a meal from Senora Gonzales' little lean-to kitchen in an alley a block west of our camp.

"You got to try her food," Flannery said. "She grills a dish of beef and vegetables with a flavor so great you don't want to chew it or swallow it. Tastes so good you just want to hold it right there in your mouth."

He was right. After eating, I overpaid, said *Gracias* and added "*Tu comida es maravillosa*" making the senora beam. A 9th Cavalry corporal told me that both in Manilla and El Paso the phrase meant her food was wonderful.

I urged the rest of the squad to try her food. Accordingly, her little business grew. The senora graduated to a small shed. I scrounged two tables and several ammo boxes for chairs.

Senora Gonzalez always seemed to rate me near the top of her list. She jovially pressed me to sample many different foods. I loved all of them … until one Sunday when I tried some of her special chili.

My God, the first spoonful was so blistering spicy I wanted to spit it out. Fearing to insult her, I tried inhaling cooling air through my blazing half-open mouth. Eyes bugged out, tears running, face streaming with sweat, I must have been a spectacle.

Someone giggled.

I managed to gulp down the blistering chili. I was still gasping when a little girl said, "Here, senor, pro favor." She handed me a soft tortilla with a big dollop of honey.

Her honey was the perfect first aid.

So was her pixie face.

She looked exactly like my sister Ellen who died seven years back. Same black hair and dancing black eyes and sweet wide smile. Now my tears ran but not because of the chili.

She and her mom and I spent the next half hour in a crazy mixture of laughs, questions in my roughshod Tex-Mex, more honey, answers in firecracker Spanish or halting English, more laughter and a final dose of honey.

Nine-year-old Maria was Senora Gonzalez' youngest. It took a while to explain that she could have been a twin to my late sister. Mother and daughter joined my tears in sympathy.

Over the next months, I almost became a household fixture at the Gonzalez kitchen. I began teaching Maria proper English and she returned the favor. She was young enough to master our "th" sound, but I never learned to trill an "R" decently.

Thinking of the wounded little girls on the bridge and remembering my sister, I fretted constantly about Maria.

With olive skin, big flashing eyes, snowy smiles and glossy black hair, most Mexican girls are beauties. But many also live in abject poverty and have few prospects. In El Paso and Juarez, at least, many seemed to end up as whores.

I mentally adopted Maria as my new kid sister and worry about her kept me awake nights.

See, Maria's mother was widowed. So with no daddy, uncle or even grandparents, Maria had no protector as she flowered into womanhood … and she had no one to finance her *quinceanera* celebration, about the only way she could hope to attract eligible bachelors.

I started a collection, putting the squeeze on men in my company. Owens, Flannery and Andy helped but others resisted. "Max, you're a chump," Simpkins said. "Give 'em that money and they'll either disappear or piss it away."

My hope was to raise $40 or $50 to finance a fifteenth birthday party with a musician or two. For safekeeping, I entrusted the fund to one of the padres at the Soccoro Mission.

I never heard how it worked out. By 1914 we were away from camp weeks at a time, chasing ghosts in Texas and New Mexico. In 1916 we began chasing Poncho Villa in the Chihuahua desert.

By 1917, the year of Maria's *quinceanera*, we were half a world away stringing barbed wire, ducking artillery and up to our butts in mud.

Maybe someday I can get back to El Paso to find how things worked out for Maria and her momma.

Chapter 10

El Paso -- 1914

Spring of 1914 in El Paso started quiet except that one March morning the town got a whole half-day of rain.

Peering out through the dripping tent flaps, Charlie Lloyd said, "That's it for this year, boys. We'll have our good ol' dust back by this afternoon."

He was right and then some. Later that same day the first trains arrived carrying the rest of the 9th Cavalry's men and mounts.

"Christ almighty," Wilson said. "I think every damned one of them horses stirs up its own sand storm. Too bad they can't water down the dirt in that stock yard."

"Oh, they do, Sam," Hart said. "They do! Just take a sniff. Every time one of them beasts turns around it lets loose with about five gallons of piss."

#

Arriving just after the cavalry was a dust-covered motor car bearing one of the stiffest men I've ever seen – Brigadier General John Pershing.

The Army nick-named him Blackjack because he once commanded both Negro cavalry and Negro infantry. But because of the way he carried himself, I thought Ramrod would be the better nickname.

"Sergeant, what do you know about our general?"

Reflecting, Owens told us, "Well fellas, I can tell you this much. I've seen Pershing up close twice.

"First time was during an inspection. The second time we came opposite ways around the corner of a building and almost bumped into one another. I jumped out of his path, saluted and said, 'Sorry, sir.'

"He just gave me a glance, saluted and kept on going.

"What struck me then and during the inspection was that his face looked froze … no, that isn't right. It looked more like somebody carved it from a big white rock. He didn't seem to have any facial motion or expression at all.

"Tough customer, I'd say. I hear tell he can be a real son of a bitch because he's very, very tight on regulations. But he's got to be a smart bastard. He's not only a West Pointer but he also graduated from law school."

Smart or not, the general sure found a way to make Congress pay attention to us. Or maybe it was that growing tension along the border was scaring Congress.

"Hey, Max, get out here and see this! We've got one of them flying machines. I can't believe my eyes!"

I sighed. "So what? We saw planes overhead five years ago at Jefferson Barracks."

Dropping my paperwork I ducked out of the tent to look at what Private Beason was so excited about. Shielding my eyes against the sun, I sure enough made out an aeroplane flying due west across El Paso … very slowly.

"Eddy," I said, "I think I could walk clear across El Paso faster than that thing is moving."

"Well, sure," Simpkins chimed in. "It's flying right into a real strong west wind."

"Well, I'm not sure it's of much use then."

Once the novelty was over, the planes didn't impress any of us. Some other things did, though.

"Wow," Sergeant Owens said. "Last month we were sucking on the hind tit, now Congress is showering us with equipment."

The trains began delivering big Dodge motor trucks. Each supposedly could carry three thousand pounds and also tow large tanks of drinking water.

Also arriving were shipments of machineguns. Some were those Colt potato-diggers but we also got Benet-Mercier guns –

manufactured by a company named Hotchkiss. Later in France we came to rely heavily on the Hotchkiss.

"These particular Benet-Merciers will be a royal pain in the ass," Sergeant Owens said. "The version that they sent us uses 7 mm ammo rather than .30-06. So that means we have to tote a separate ammo supply for them, otherwise they're junk."

The new guns were peculiar in that they fired from strips rather than fabric belts like the Colt. "They sent us strips for both twenty-four or thirty catridges," the sergeant explained.

"You hand-load catridges into the strips, snapping them into their grooves one-by-one. It takes time, so before any action you'd best have a cart full of them strips all loaded and ready to go.

"The good thing about these guns," he said, "is that they got these cooling fins, so you can shoot them a lot before they overheat. One guy aims and fire while his pard just feeds the loaded strips in one side and pulls the empties out t'other."

We had to help expand Camp Cotton to accommodate the 16th Infantry Regiment, part of the Army's entire Eighth Brigade also en route from California.

Train loads of soldiers disembarked daily for ten days. Instead of our original lonely line of forty tents along Paisano Drive, Camp Cotton became a small tent city extending all the way southeast near to Cordova Island in the Rio Grande.

The bulk of the brigade settled in at Fort Bliss, an old Civil War post north of town. It easily accommodated the rest of the brigade of about four thousand men.

# # #

"Damn! This is one hell of a build-up," First Sergeant O'Neill told us. "I been in this Army since the Indian wars but I ain't never seen so many troops in one place. Something's really stirring."

"Crazy thing, though. No sooner do we get a new company here than one of the others marches right out of town."

Lieutenant Creek told us General Pershing, a veteran of the Indian war, was doing as Sherman and Sheridan had done in the last century – scattering garrisons in hostile country. He posted company-strength units all along the Mexican-American border.

Their job was to intercept or break up increasing numbers of raids by Villa's troops.

Some garrisons were lucky to be put up in towns where they could shelter from the winter winds. Most of them, however, had to requisition extra sets of long underwear when they camped on the border opposite Mexican towns like Josefa Ortiz or La Linaea.

We heard Pershing planned to supply garrisons by truck. But I thought mules were far more reliable. Aside from breaking down regularly, the trucks had real thin tires which sank deep both in sand and mud -- provided we actually found roads rather than trails.

More than once I found myself saying, "Okay, men. Out! Get busy! Unload everything and then we'll push her across this creek bed."

We always had to unload heavy reels of telegraph wire. General Pershing wanted to be in constant touch with his garrisons.

Unfortunately, Americans and Mexicans alike took a liking to the wire. No sooner would we connect headquarters with, say, Columbus, than operators would report the lines dead.

It got so I could count on the platoon commander telling me almost every day, "Corporal, take your squad and look for the latest line break. Some yahoo along the border probably helped himself to one or two hundred yards of wire … or he cut it to make trouble for Uncle Sam."

So we could only rely fitfully on telegraph. But our most reliable aid was a group of Apache scouts.

"I sometimes wonder about them scouts," Owens told me. "They're hard to read and they never have much to say. After the way we've treated their people it's hard to believe they don't hate our guts. But they sure as shit hate Mexicans."

"I've gotten to know one of them," I said. "Old Joseph Whitehat. His face reminds me of those photos of Geronimo. Looks like it's carved from mahogany.

"Like you say, he never talks much. But he sure can read the ground. He just looks up, points and says, 'Mex,' and sure enough, you find 'em just over the next rise.

"And when you look at him in surprise, he just gives about half a grin."

# # #

"Our main worry," the company commander told us, "is that Villa's troops might start raiding in large numbers."

"Why would they do that, Sir? There ain't that much to steal from these ranches."

"That's not the point, corporal. Villa's in a rage that our government gave a lot of help to some rival of his."

The first real attack came in November.

Villa's men assaulted the border town of Nogales but found out that it was like tackling a cactus.

The Nogales garrison was alert and met the assault with rifle and machinegun fire.

The rebels backed off.

Chapter 11

El Paso -- Early 1916

"This is a hell of a way to bring in the new year," Lieutenant Creek told us. "You can practically hear the whole damned brigade growling."

The men's anger arose over a story that, after his rebuff at Nogales, Pancho Villa halted a train in Chihuahua and slaughtered dozens of American passengers, including women and children.

By January 20, however, new accounts toned down. Now they reported Villa actually killed neither ladies nor children, but sixteen men, employees of an American mining company in Mexico.

We mulled it over in the NCO tent.

"I don't care how many Americans that little weasel killed or didn't kill," the first sergeant said, "we're still going to have to go after him."

Sergeant Owens took a sip of his beer, "Oh, Top, I don't think so," he said. "According to Max here, the papers report that he killed those miners way down in Santa Isabel. That's a couple hundred miles or so due south … quite a piece inside Mexico, you understand. Do you think we're about to invade another country?"

"Well, why not, by God?" O'Neill snapped. "We did it once before and whipped them hands down."

"Yep," I countered, "but that was more'n sixty years ago. The Mexicans didn't have much of an army then while officers like Stonewall Jackson and Longstreet were leading our troops, and all run by Winfield Scott."

"Lookee here, Max," O'Neill said. "You can be readin' all them history books you want. But in case you didn't notice, a couple of years back Germany invaded France! So why shouldn't we be doin' the like with Mexico?"

"Well, Sarge," Owens said, "how about because now Germany has a hellish big war on its hands? At least six other countries I can name are fighting them. I don't think the president or Congress wants a war with Mexico, and that's what you'd get."

O'Neill snorted and chugged the last of his brew. "Well, Christ Almighty, fellas, we can't just sit by and let this Villa bastard butcher Americans, now can we?"

I got up to open three new beers.

"You know, I think the first sergeant's got a point," I said. "We should run the bastard to ground. We're trained and tough. We've got good weapons. We could handle any band of mestizos that Pancho Villa sends against us."

"Damn right, Max!" the first shirt said, taking a deep swallow.

Owens grinned and said, "Well, maybe half right. If Villa attacked us, we'd wipe him out.

"But Villa's cagey. He won't attack us. He'll stick to murdering civilians. For us to try catching him on his own ground would be useless. He knows the land. He's lived all his life in Chihuahua. We don't know the area at all."

"Well, I see your point," I said. "So how about contributing a couple of bucks to Maria's *quinceanera?*"

"You bastard! How many times you gonna hit me up for that?"

"As many as it takes, Sarge."

# # #

About all we did through the rest of January and February was talk, patrol and guard the supply runs to General Pershing's border garrisons. Little pin-prick raids continued here and there. I figured some of them were just ordinary bandits taking advantage of the revolution's turmoil.

But on Friday morning, March 10, I had to give my squad some bad news. "Okay, boys, all weekend passes are cancelled!"

"What the hell?" Flannery yelled. "I had big plans for tonight. Been saving up for it."

"Too bad, Mike. Headquarters just put us on alert. We're all confined to post."

"What's going on?"

"Beats the hell out of me but I'd bet five bucks it's got something to do with Villa."

No takers.

Early in the afternoon, Lieutenant Creek called a meeting of NCOs to give us the word.

"Late last night," he said, "Pancho Villa led several hundred raiders across the border and attacked Columbus. They burned most of the town and killed twenty-two Americans, among them eight members of the 13th Cav plus a lady who was with child."

We all looked at each other. "Oh, boy," Sergeant Owens said. "That tears it."

"Correct," the lieutenant said. He went on, "You'll be happy to know that after the first assault, the Cavalry got their machineguns out and knocked the raiders for a loop. They killed about a hundred and pursued the survivors back across the border. Captured a dozen of them."

"Sir," O'Neill asked, "how many raiders was there?"

"The cavalry believes about five hundred."

"By God, I bet we go after Villa now," the first shirt said. "The president and congress won't stand for them raiding an American town and killing American citizens."

# # #

In a week, at the president's direction, General Pershing put the brigade on the move into Chihuahua. I waved goodbye to Maria from the back of a truck that convoyed us eighty miles to Columbus.

At first, Creed's company of skirmishers crossed the border on foot and headed south. It was desert, but at first a fortunate west wind blew the dust across our path and away from of our faces.

"I can't believe this," Sergeant Owens said "It's like the ancient Israelites following pillars of smoke. Except that here they're dust clouds ... clouds that alert Villa."

Far ahead of us, we saw dust clouds kicked up by several troops of cavalry. They were aching to capture Villa, our expedition's primary mission, or to kill him.

I think General Pershing knew what he was doing, because he had several columns headed different routes into Villa's country.

But as the army was set up then, Supply was a separate department that wasn't under the general's control. And though it was springtime, Chihuahua's flatlands were arid and hot and nobody was getting to us with beans, bullets or water.

The Mexican government wouldn't let us use their railways and Supply's trucks usually broke down on sunken foot-wide trails lined with head-size rocks.

General Pershing ordered the Engineers to turn trails into roads.

Until that worked out, we had to make do with iron rations. They came in a cube-shaped tin box -- three buillion cakes mixed with wheat and three bars of sweetened chocolate.

"The chocolate is okay," Simpkins said. "But these damned cakes taste like dust."

"You chowderhead, you're supposed to mix them with water as a soup or a stew."

"Yeah, well corp, we're a little short on water right now, ain't we?"

We also carried our basic load of ammo, of course – hundred-round bandoleers of .30-06 in five-round stripper clips.

# # #

The men of Lieutenant Creek's company saw almost no action during the so-called Punitive Expedition.

During our first week into Chihuahua, we heard several bullets sing among us.

"Who's shooting at us?"

"Can't tell. Can't see a soul through them heatwaves."

At one point, we managed to get on the flank of a Villa firing line, forcing them to vamoose. That was near Colonia Dublan, the town which became the expedition's headquarters and base.

The 16th Infantry spent the rest of the expedition dying of boredom near a town called El Valle.

# # #

When we weren't in a dust storm, the sky above us was cobalt blue. The land was yellowish, dotted everywhere with small clusters of brush or cactus. The sun hammered us so hard that the Mexicans' sombreros suddenly made sense. See, they created wide *sombre* which I found out was Spanish 'shade'.

At least El Valle was near a river with luxuriant trees and shrubs along the banks. We fashioned mud brick huts for ourselves and patrolled into the adjoining hills.

"Funny thing," Sergeant Owens said.

"What's that, Sarge?"

"Well, I been talking with some Mexicans hereabouts. They all hate Villa. The claim they want him captured and hanged, or at least jailed."

"Well, that's good."

"No, it isn't because they hate us gringos just as much, so they won't tell where he hides or what he's doing. I think we're going to have a hell of a time finding him."

We never did.

In fact, we spent the most of the expedition conducting meaningless patrols and trying to keep from going stir-crazy. The so-called Punitive Expedition was strictly a cavalry show.

In February 1917, we weren't surprised to receive orders to march back north. We marched and rode a touch over four hundred miles to cross the Rio Grande back into Texas.

That's when the boredom came to a halt.

Chapter 12

El Paso -- 1917

When we returned to El Paso, the entire town – not to mention Camp Cotton and Fort Bliss – was in a boiling fury. It had to do with something called the Zimmerman Telegram.

It didn't take long for everyone to fill us in. The battalion's supply sergeant, who never left El Paso, explained it.

"What happened was that the goddamn Kaiser sent a secret message to Mexico's govmint saying if Mexico went to war agin' us then Germany'd help Mexico get back its old territories, Arizona, New Mexico and, for Christ's sake, Kansas."

"Kansas? Shit, we never took Kansas from Mexico!"

"I know that! I bet Zimmerman meant Texas."

He said all this news came out when the British broke the German diplomatic code, read the Kaiser's mail and released its contents to Congress and President Wilson.

Like everyone else, we found the story both funny and infuriating.

Sergeant Owens said, "And I suppose Kaiser Bill wants to set up Pancho Villa as governor of the whole damn Southwest."

"Governor Pancho, eh? That's rich. Let 'em try."

First Sergeant O'Neill, however, looked grave about the news.

"Washington won't put up with this crap," he said. "It probably means we'll go to war with the Germans. I hear they's just about the toughest enemy you can face this side of the Comanches. The Fritzes have stood off the French, the English and Italy and they've just about knocked Russia out of the war."

"Do you suppose General Pershing will show up soon and give us the final word?"

"Nope," Lieutenant Creek said. "The general's gone. He's headed off to Washington. I think they might have a big job for him…and for us."

# # #

In the evenings over the next week, I enjoyed quiet reunions with Maria and Senora Gonzalez – plus several excellent meals. "So, Senor Max! You come back tomorrow? Momma will fix new food for you."

"Mrs. Gonzalez, and Maria, I'm sorry but I found out today I cannot come back for a while. All of a sudden, we are very, very busy. We have no time. And soon we may leave."

"You go to Chihuahua again?"

"No, Senora. All I know is that sometime we will leave Texas."

A few mornings later, all passes were stopped. Lieutenant Creek gave me an hour off post to say goodbye.

"The two of you have been my family," I said. Senora Gonzalez hugged me and kissed me on each cheek. Then I gave Maria a bear hug. "*Mi hermana pequeña,* I will miss you so much." I started weeping and Maria asked if I had eaten chili, so we were able to laugh.

But my tears started flowing again right down into my moustache as I walked away, *Viaja con dios* echoing in my ears.

# # #

"Men, before long our regiment is loading up and headed to New Jersey. When we get there, Company B will grow in size. And the 16th Regiment will double in size.

"The War Department is expanding each company in the army from a hundred seventy-four rifles to at least two hundred."

Meanwhile, he said the Department also would augment each regiment with something brand new -- a machine-gun battalion.

"Men, that means the regiment will have eighteen heavy machineguns, each with a crew of nine. What's more, each infantry squad will have two smaller automatic weapons.

"And to show another big change, Supply now will come directly under the commander's control. Each regiment will have its own supply company and its mission is to keep all of us fed, armed and supplied with ammo.

"So you can see," the lieutenant said, "this man's army is going to grow very big very fast. As part of that growth, we'll receive a lot of new men with very little training."

"Well, we know what that means," the first sergeant said.

"You're right, First Sergeant O'Neill," the lieutenant said. "It means training, training, training and more training. But I can tell you right now, the 16th Infantry is going to be gutted!"

"Gutted? Whoa, sir! How d'you mean that?"

He explained half of the 16th's experienced officers and non-coms – like other regular army regiments -- would be reassigned to camps all over the country to help train the flood of raw recruits.

"They'll leave half of us behind as this regiment's cadre. It'll be our job to bring our new people up to measure. Oh, and it also means promotions for all of us."

"What do you mean, sir?"

"First Sergeant O'Neill, I'm advised that you'll become a regimental sergeant major. Your job will be to support and ride herd on the fairly new NCOs as they put recruits through their paces.

"Sergeant Owens, you'll become a battalion sergeant major but I'm not sure which battalion, yet. And you, Corporal Coleman are about to become a sergeant."

"Sir," I raised a hand, "I have a question: will you be getting your railroad tracks?"

"No, I'll never make captain."

All of us groaned at the injustice of it.

He yelled "Surprise!" and grinned. "They're jumping me to major. I'll probably wind up as a battalion exec."

We cheered and applauded.

"Thanks, men. Now hold it down! Listen, this is going to be very, very difficult for all of us. We're entering what I call a crush program. We old hands have to train hundreds of thousands of civilians to march, dive for cover, salute, shoot and kill.

"To do that, the army needs a lot more NCOs, so give me the names of your people who could lead a squad or maybe even platoon."

"I don't know about that, sir."

"Look, Max, you run a squad of ten men. Every damned one of them knows his drill. They're tough even if they haven't seen combat. Most of them shoot well. They've all marched and patrolled for several hundred miles now so none is a tenderfoot.

"So they're soldiers which is more than you can say for these green kids who'll get drafted into our ranks. I've got to believe at least five of your squad know enough and are tough enough to train recruits. So get those names to me."

"Yessir!"

"Now look, I hear that before this summer is over the 16th is one of four regiments that will ship to France. Together we'll comprise the First Infantry Division. So you can see we've got a hell of a lot to do in a very short time."

The thought of running a platoon all by myself was scary but also exciting. I could just see myself as kind of a buffer between forty-five restless, bitching soldiers and their commanding officer.

I never had much of a chance to dwell on it. I didn't even have time to plan how I would handle my new duties. Too much happened too fast to the whole Army.

In fact, it gave me a grim sort of comfort to realize that almost everybody else in the U.S. Army faced the same problems and uncertainties.

For instance, General Pershing was undergoing a big, big jump in rank. Instead of a mere brigade, he now was to command all the American forces in Europe.

One of his early command decisions was to pick us – the 16th Infantry Regiment -- to lead the American Expeditionary Force to France.

Some jealous jerk in the 28th Infantry griped that with the 16th leading, the initials AEF should stand for Ass End Forward.

On our last night Major Creek gave me permission to use a truck.

 I drove it to deliver $78 to Maria's priest at Soccoro Mission. I could have paid a last call on Maria and her mother, but I didn't want the pain.

Late that night Company B boarded the Missouri Pacific for New Jersey.

Of course, in the Army Way of things, the train didn't pull out until dawn.

Chapter 13

Camp Dix -- 1917

As I've said, the training wasn't near as tough as in the Old Army.

But maybe it didn't need to be.

The men and boys who came into my company at Camp Dix in New Jersey actually *wanted* to be soldiers. They were excited to learn to march and fire rifles. They considered joining the 16th Infantry to be an honor. They were burning to capture Berlin and kill Kaiser Bill.

One of them also made a stab at killing Andy McKinnis, now reinstated as a corporal.

Before I assigned McKinnis to train a platoon of recruits, I warned him. "Corporal, these boys aren't a bunch of dumb laborers from the stock yards like Hart and me. They're sharp and smart and I don't believe they'll cotton to insults about their mothers. Or being called dipshits."

Perhaps he simply resented taking orders from me. He sneered. "Ahh, they're just babies that still want their sugar titties!"

"Fair warning, Corporal!"

McKinnis didn't listen. Next day he called one of the recruits, a Princeton student, a slop bucket. The recruit chuckled and said, "Hello, contents."

The insult went over McKinnis's head, but other recruits' roaring laughter enraged him. He struck the recruit with his swagger stick and the next instant found himself flat on the parade ground with his dentures five feet away.

It took some doing, but I convinced our new company commander, Captain Felton, to go easy on the recruit.

I explained that in France he'd probably be worth ten of McKinnis. For one thing, the lad happened to speak and read both French and German. Second, he was champion of the university's rifle team. Third, he was eager to fight Germans.

"Sir," I said, "by contrast I don't think McKinnis can do much more than conduct drills and carry a rifle. Besides, he just seems to hate most of his comrades. Our army's growing but he can't seem to grow"

Captain Felton fined the recruit and gave him a royal dressing down – but nothing compared to the private ass-chewing to which he subjected McKinnis while refusing his demands to court martial the recruit.

After he burnished both men, the captain called me into his office and looked at me thoughtfully. "Sergeant, just how much schooling do you have?"

"Only my mom's one-room school," I said.

"Through what grade?"

"Well, we didn't really have grades, sir. We all worked together with the older kids helping to teach the little ones. I was just twelve when typhoid took her and my father."

"Sorry to hear about that," he said. "Give me an idea of how far you went in mathematics."

"We were just starting algebra, sir, when mother died. And I've kind of kept up with it. I like it and geometry."

"What was your hardest book?"

"I finished Thucydides while we were in Chihuahua."

"In Greek?"

"On no, sir. A British translation. I only have English and some Tex-Mex."

"Hmm. Okay, sergeant, carry on and make damn sure your recruits don't bust any more NCOs."

"Sir!"

# # #

The reason we had to depend upon occasional idiots like McKinnis was that the War Department ballooned all regiments, including the 16th Infantry. We grew from seven hundred men to two thousand.

At the same time, the department transferred half of our original seven hundred officers, NCOs and riflemen to train entirely new regiments at other centers around the country. The remaining three hundred fifty old soldiers in the 16th then got the job of training almost seventeen hundred brand new recruits.

Down on my echelon, this meant promoting and relying on members of my old squad. Solid soldiers like Andy Hart, Mike Flannery, Willie DeVries and Sam Wilson became the sergeants of Company B's platoons.

My job was to guide the old hands in their work and so the regiment promoted me another grade – to first sergeant.

Fortunately, the new recruits were so eager to learn so that our despite own inexperience even jerks like McKinnis couldn't dampen their enthusiasm.

"Top," Captain Felton told me, "these are good troops. Or they will be. They've kept up their spirits even though some of them still are drilling in their saddle oxfords or even bare feet. The Quartermaster Corps is having a hell of a hard time providing complete unforms for this flood of new recruits."

The army just wasn't ready for one million draftees let alone four million.

Oh, the Corps of Engineers did a fantastic job fixing up old Spanish-American war camps for hundreds of thousands of trainees. But at least at first, the Quartermaster Corps seemed overwhelmed.

The new men complained, and I couldn't blame them.

"Sarge, when in the hell is the Army gonna give us boots and uniforms like yours? These oxfords of mine just don't handle the mud very well."

Neither did their civilian trousers. But compared to the bitching my trainees and I did back in 1909, the new people seemed fairly patient. As the surge of new recruits reached its peak, we NCOs received a crisp lecture from Major Akree, executive officer of the training battalion

"Men, our focus here at Camp Dix must be physical fitness first, then drill and, third, marksmanship.

"The real training, the training for combat, will come only after we arrive in France. Our instructors will be Englishmen, Aussies or Poilus.

"Sir, what are Pwa-loos?"

"Poilu is the nickname for your ordinary French soldier. It means something like 'hairy one' or maybe you could say 'ape.'

"The key thing," he said, "is that there's so much we don't know about the war in France. And so we're going to have to learn from our allies how to dig into mother earth just like those armadillos we saw in Texas."

For a brief time we got an ape of our own, a thick-set Scottish infantryman whom the British Army lent to the U.S. Army for training purposes.

"Gentlemen, Ah'm Color Sergeant Angus MacLausen of the Highland Light Infantry. Ah've been invited here to give you a wee picture of the way we fight the Huns on the Western Front."

"Well, sergeant, fighting is fighting."

"Ah'm forced to disagree," he said. "It may strain your credulity," he added with a grin, "but fighting in yon trenches is rarely aboot rifles. When ye get tore intae the Huns, ye want tae carry the likes of shovels, pistols, cudgels, bayonets or even one of these."

He held up a set of brass knuckles with a six-inch blade jutting to one side.

"Ye can wear it on either hand, o' course. I recommend having them made wi' the knife tae the right so that if ye miss when ye punch, ye can stab on t' way back. Quite eefficient they are."

I said, "I've got to get me one of them."

The boys exchanged shocked looks. What was the point of being able to hit a target at three hundred yards?

"Tae be sure," MacLausen said, "ye'll aye rely on machine guns, as many as ye can get. But there's muir yet. Ye must learn to live in the earth and how tae keep your feet dry when you spend days on end in a bog.

"At times, too, the German Imperial Army will test your endurance. Ye must be able tae maintain your composure during a four-day artillery barrage upon your position," he said. "That's aboot a hundred hours … *steady* hours … of artillery pounding. "And be ready at all times to don your gas respirator … gas mask, I believe you Yanks call it … and still be prepared meanwhile to repel an infantry attack."

"A four-day barrage? My God."

"Aye, and Ah'm cairtain such will call to mind many of your childhood prayers. In addition to prayer, Ah recommend ye practice several times daily in donning gas masks. It's a thing you want to do automatically. So practice constantly."

"Sergeant, why do you call the Germans 'Huns'?"

"Ooch, it's no us what gave them the name.

"Back when yon bluidy bastard Kaiser sent troops tae help us fight China's Boxer Rebellion, he ordered his soldiers to take nae prisoners. His exact words were, tae be as pitiless as the Hun invaders of Christian Rome.

"When invading Belgium in '14, the Germans conducted themselves Hun-like too. Ye might say they earned the name and it stuck."

# # #

We endlessly practiced donning gas masks which our farm boys called nosebags. Fourth Platoon challenged the other platoons to a baseball tournament … while wearing our gaspirators on a 90-degee day.

The main rule was you had to keep your mask on at all times. That included umpires, baseline coaches and spectators. Team managers had to wear masks when protesting umpires' calls. Take off your mask and the ump throws you out of the game.

I appointed Corporal Flannery to be Second Platoon's manager and Second Platoon won the tournament.

The captain congratulated us. Saying that with pitchers, hitters and catchers masked and equally sight-handicapped it was no surprise that the scores, Earned Run Averages and Batting Averages all approached zero.

Among other things the masked tournament taught us:

Mask-related foul-ups cause much laughter.

Laughter leads to choking. Running hard when masked leads to choking.

A swing and a miss could dislodge the mask giving one's face an instant of cool relief.

Fielders slammed into each other when chasing the final game's three pop-up flies.

A masked pitcher has a hard time trying to pick off a stealing runner.

Masked baseball never became popular with players or fans.

Chapter 14

Hoboken, New Jersey -- 1917

As we filed up the gangway into the *S.S. Leviathan* I muttered, "I'm not looking forward to this."

Blackwell in front of me said, "Oh, Sarge, I think it's keen. Never been on a really big boat before. I wonder how long it will take us to get to France."

"Keen! *Keen?* We'll see how keen you think it is by the time we arrive. But I'd guess it'll take maybe ten days. But, believe me, Blackie, it's going to seem longer."

"Sarge is right," Simpkins said. "A lot of guys are gonna get sick and that's going to make almost everybody else flash their hash. Believe me, I've been at sea and I know. You watch!"

As we wound down the ladders into the hold, the heat and fuel oil odor hit us together. "Wow, that's strong," I said. "But it isn't near as bad as the stock yards."

Simpkins chuckled. "It will be."

Wilson widened his eyes comically. "Boys, it's kind of like going into the belly of a whale."

Beason said, "What the hell are you talking about?"

"Can't you feel it? The vibration? It's kind of like a giant living creature, big as a whale … lots bigger, in fact."

Ulrich said, "For Pete's sake, Wilson, it's just the ship's machinery. It keeps the lights on and the fans running down here so's we don't all strangulate."

As we began descending the third ladder, our line came to a stop. Blocking us because he was trying to climb back topside was Private Rozanov. Face gray and sweaty, he said, "I can't take this. Gotta get out of here and right now!"

It took Davies, Blackwell and me a few minutes to calm him down. As we resumed our descent into the ship. Blackwell, a college boy, said entering the ship's holds reminded him of the Divine Comedy.

"Nothing comic about it," Simpkins retorted. "It's so hot it's like hiking down into hell."

"That's what I'm saying," Blackwell said.

"You didn't say anything of the sort," Simpkins snapped.

"Yes I did. The narrative poem by Dante Aligheri talks about descending into hell."

"Oh, I read that," Rozanov said. "Very Catholic isn't it?"

"Well, of course…"

"Guys! Guys!" I said. "I love a good book, too, but just save the literary crap for later. Let's get organized down here."

The constant jabber seemed typical of the new guys, nervous in novel surroundings. We regular army types just accepted it and started pushing the kids away from the ladder. "Bunk by squads and stow your gear over there inside the nets on the hatch cover."

"Good Lord, they expect us to sleep on these canvas bunks?"

"Of course not, Liddle. Didn't you know we ordered a genuine feather mattress especially for you?"

Fortunately, the hold was well lit so squad members spotted each other easily and clustered together among the tiers of canvas bunks.

After Hart and I stowed our gear, we explored. We found a locker where the ship's crew thoughtfully stowed lots of mops and buckets.

"I got a feeling we're going to need those," Hart said.

"Let's just not think about it right now, okay?"

Just then the battalion sergeant major came half-way down the hold's ladder. He bellowed, "Quiet down and pay attention!"

Then he yelled, "I said SHUT UP!"

In the subsequent quiet he said, "Now, goddammit, listen to your corporals and sergeants. They'll take you through lifeboat drills and keep you at it until it's an organized, quiet movement to the outer decks. No confusion, grab-assing or screwing around!

"Understand? This ship ain't leaving the dock until the captain is happy with your lifeboat drills."

# # #

The sergeant major's orders worked. It only took two rehearsals for our company to join the rest of the battalion topside in orderly gatherings near the boats and rafts.

As we filed back below decks, one of the kids turned to me. "Sarge, this time I think we got it right. Ran just like a grade school fire drill, eh?"

"Yep. Went pretty smooth. Now, what's your name?"

"I'm Bill Adamczak."

"Oh, yeah! You're the hothead who hit the corporal's false teeth for a home run." He looked about fifteen. "I recall you were a university student, but where's your home?"

"I'm from Chicago."

"Ha. Ever tour the stockyards?"

"Nah, we lived on the north side. My dad did business at the yards, though. He's in shipping."

"Livestock?"

"Yes."

"Well, at one time maybe I was one of his workers. Some years back I worked in there in what you might call the ham and bacon business."

Quietly he said, "Well, we'll soon be in business with the *Deutches Heer*."

"The what?"

"That's the German term for the Kaiser's imperial army. So they're shipping us to our own slaughter. Sort of…"

I broke in. "Look, you're out of line, Adamczak. We're the ones who'll do the slaughtering. You just keep that in mind, okay?"

"Right, Sarge, I hope you're right."

So did I.

# # #

The *Leviathan* got underway next morning and I think by noon she lost maybe ten tons of cargo. I refer to breakfasts spewed over the sides by four or five thousand seasick soldiers.

Somebody else gets to tell the tale of our voyage. All I care to report is that no Imperial German submarine sank us. I kept busy trying to keep troops busy so that the seasickness, the smell, the vomit on the decks, all would seem to pass faster.

Not that our arrival in Saint Nazaire ended it all. Unloading moved at a snail's pace.

Too few dock workers were available and most of them looked like tottery old men.

Chapter 15

France -- 1917

"Hey, Top, if you thought unloading the ship was slow, what about them cramming the men into this little train?"

Sergeant Hart was complaining to me as if I had the power to do anything about it.

"What the hell, Andy? Do you expect me to take it up with Pershing? Is that it? Be thankful we're out in clean air after being cooped up in that damned ship."

"Sorry, Max. I just had to get if off my chest. At least the folks here seem nice."

We were the first troops of the American Expeditionary Force to arrive in France … and Pershing's favorite regiment, at that.

Without exception, French folk at Saint Nazaire welcomed us, men and women alike. They grinned. They waved. Some cried. They yelled "OoooRAH!" which I think meant "Hurray." There even was something about "Viva the Teddies!" whatever that may have meant.

However, our company commander, Captain Bowcher, became embroiled in a furious argument with a uniformed French official. Adamczak translated for them, speaking quietly, but the conversation became more and more heated until the captain and his counterpart were shouting. And as he shouted, the Frenchman violently flailed his hands and arms.

Finally, the official gave a dramatic shrug, sneered at Captain Bowcher, and stalked away.

"Yeah, they're nice people," Wilson said, "but it's damned unfriendly of them to cram us into these gawdawful things."

He was grousing – just as Captain Bowcher had been -- about the miniature box cars, fifty to a train, in which they were taking us to the French interior. According to their labels – *Hommes 40 Chevaus 8* -- the little cars were designed to carry either eight horses or forty men.

The little railway cars stank of horse piss and dung. Of course they contained neither seats nor benches. And no one was about to stretch out on the well-manured floor

In disgust, Wilson said, "I think the last time around somebody got confused. Instead of forty men, they loaded forty horses into this particular car. And never bothered to muck it out!"

He started kicking horse dung from the car, breaking up those brown apples into a fine dust which arose toward out faces.

DeVries said, "Sam, will you quit that? And quit your belly-aching? All that stuff on the floor is gonna put a fine shine on your boots."

"Horse shit, Willie!"

"Hold on, Sam! I'm not kidding. Look, everybody knows the shoeshine boys on Chicago's north side use horse apples to preserve shoe leather and to put a great shine on it. Isn't that right, Sarge?"

"Sorry, private," I said. "I never got to Chicago's north side. I shine my boots with polish, so I think you're feeding Sam a line of bullshit."

"Well anyway," Simpkins asked, "where are we going in these pungent conveyances?"

I pointed to a map they issued me. "We're probably on a seven or eight hour trip – roughly three hundred miles -- due east to a town named Gondrecourt. That'll be our training center. We'll spend six weeks there learning how to fight the Fritzes "

"Uh, Sarge," Adamczak said, "I don't think that's how the natives pronounce it."

"What, the word 'Fritzes?'"

No, Sarge, I'm talking about our destination. It's more like *Gone Ruh Cour*."

Speaking from the creaky age of twenty-four to a mere 20-year-old, I said, "Okay, lad, you're the French speaker. So from this moment on, I rely on you to help us say the names on French signs and maps. So what's the right way to pronounce the port we're leaving?"

"It's *Say Nazar*, Sarge."

# # #

Fortunately, yard-wide head-level drop panels gave the box cars ample ventilation. Once the train began moving, we could breathe fresh countryside air laced with locomotive soot and the fragrance of half-dried dung.

We didn't arrive at Gondrecourt until dawn. It took most of the morning to reassemble companies that had been broken up to ship us in groups of forty, regardless of unit.

Knowing our travels had whipped us, the Army directed us to our barracks, local farmers' barns.

We spread our blankets in the hay on the second floors, leaving the ground levels to horses, milk cows and – in our barn – a family of kittens who mewed for hours on end.

I couldn't sleep because of the kittens' noise and because so much was swirling in my mind.

Gotta get a steady supply of chlorine for the water. Even the French don't drink their own water. Without chlorine the troops need to drink wine and won't that be a fine mess? Half will get stinking drunk.

Got to read up on aiming Stokes Mortars. And remember MacLausen stressing bayonets – train so much that ye go by instinct, men. Double advance! High guard! Butt stroke. Low guard! Retire. Advance.

I finally slept, but somebody stirring about 0400 awakened me. Two men crouched at one of the barn's dormers peering out into the night.

One whispered, "Oh, my God! Would you harken to that?"

I threw off my blanket, got up and leaned over them. "What's up?"

"The war," Davies said.

"Hear that thud, thump, thump, Sarge?" Simpkins said, "I bet a fin it's artillery. You can see the flashes now and then. Looks like heat lightning. It's the Western Front and somebody's catching hell."

"Get some sleep." I said.

Simpkins said, "With all that in mind I can't sleep."

"Better get used to it," I said. "Next month we'll be in the line and those shells will be exploding all around us."

"Then the initials AEF will stand for the Anus End Flatulent," Davies said.

Nobody laughed.

Chapter 16

Gondrecourt -- 1917

The following day, a major from AEF headquarters handed us over to a cadre of officers and NCOs from the 47th *Chasseurs a Pied Alpins*.

In introducing us, he said the French regiment were known as the Blue Devils not merely because of their uniform colors but also because they'd beat the hell out of Germans who tried invading the Voges mountains.

Leading them was a one-eyed colonel with what seemed like a razor-sharp tongue.

Our translator, Adamczak told us more. "That title of theirs, *Chasseur a Pied* word-for-word means 'Hunters on Foot.' But from what they tell me, they actually are light infantry who trained and specialized in mountain fighting."

"Their outfits sure look like what the old Union Army wore," Flannery said.

"My granddaddy kept his uniform in mothballs," he added, "and it looked pretty much the same -- dark blue jacket and powder blue pants. Those hats, though … great big, flat, floppy things. They look more like something women should wear."

"Yeah," Beason said. "Looks like they're wearing big blueberry pies on their heads"

"Hey, you dingbat," Rozanov said, "those hats are called berets. They're very common all over Europe."

"Yeah well, I'll tell you, I'm never trading my campaign hat for one of them pies."

As it happened, we all had to trade in our wide-brimmed campaign hats.

In their place the Army issued the fore-and-aft overseas cap.

Supply Services also issued us those British wash-basin steel helmets. The helmets had straps inside which you could adjust to your head size.

Those weren't the only changes.

When our ship left the dock in New Jersey, we only had enough Springfield rifles for the regiment's original strength of seven hundred men.

Once we got to Gondrecourt, the Army issued 1917 Enfield rifles to our other thirteen hundred troops.

The people who got them, of course, immediately griped. "Sarge, these rifles are too heavy! Their action ain't as smooth as the '03, either. And they got these strange looking sights."

My job was to sell the troops on the new weapon. I explained the Enfield to be of solid British design and manufacture with few differences from the Springfield.

"Look, men, its bolt has the same double locking lugs and the same long extractor as the '03. And it's chambered for exactly the same cartridge as the Springfield, the .30-06.

"One of the few real differences is that the Enfield has flip-up leaf sights instead of the '03's ladder sights. And that dog-legged bolt handle puts your cocking hand closer to the trigger. Instead of a five-bullet magazine, the Enfield has room for six cartridges.

"Until you get used to it, the Enfield's action seems stiffer because it cocks when you close the bolt while the '03 cocks on opening. But here's the only thing that matters, men – as I said, it shoots the exact same cartridge as the Springfield and that's what kills Huns.

Beason said, "I don't care, Sarge, I just don't like its looks."

"Beason, where are you from?"

"Virginia, Sarge."

"Well, you being a southerner ought to have a special place in your heart for the Enfield. See, Enfield, an English manufacturer, provided most of the rifles for the Confederacy."

"Oh. But I still don't like its looks."

"You're breaking my heart, Joe. You'll find out on the range that it's a damn fine firearm. But I'll tell you what, young trooper, you *will* carry the Enfield when on the march.

"If you don't want it when we get into combat, fine! Just throw it away and try fighting the Fritzes bare-handed."

We only took the new rifles to the range twice.

After their initial grousing, men who trained with Springfields grudgingly accepted the Enfield. They eventually came to swear by it.

One draftee, a shy little kid named Fothergill, printed some beautiful shots at eight hundred yards with his Enfield.

When I congratulated him, he tried to say thanks but couldn't. His stammer made it impossible.

Once we started training in earnest with the Blue Devils, they put kind of a damper on things.

They told us we'd do very little long-range shooting when in the trenches.

Lieutenant Henri Barbier opened our training by saying, "Your bayonet and rifle butt, she is much more important in trenches.

"When those mordant Bosche jump into your position two meters away, you need no long-range sight. You shoot as you say from zee 'ip? Like zee bookskin cowboys."

"What?"

I snapped, "Dammit Wilson! Pay attention! He's saying you 'Shoot from the hip'."

"Oh."

The lieutenant turned our platoon over to a gorilla-shaped sergeant named Lavigne who vaguely reminded me of Corporal McKinnis. But instead of drilling us endlessly on Attention and At Ease, his specialty was endless demands that we hit the dirt again and again and again.

"You men shall be obliged to fall flat so zee Boche *feu* – the whizz-bam, you call it -- cannot strike you. Now, fall! *Vite!* Quickly! Or you are dead!"

We went flat.

Lavigne wanted us even flatter. He shouted, "*Tomber a plat*! *Pieds a plat*!"

"Adamzcak! What's he's saying?"

"He's saying to drop and to keep your feet flat to the ground. It's so German fire doesn't hit your heels. He says to keep your head and your ass low so they don't get hit, either."

The sergeant strolled about, shouting and kicking the boot soles of troops who didn't get the word.

Soon I found myself trying to repeat his order, "Veetay! Tombair! Peedsaplah, dammit! That means drop fast. Feet flat! Get it?"

With Adamczak's aid, the sergeant explained that we must stay low and worm our way toward the enemy. The sergeant laughed, "You must be like zee serpent of *la Bible*, and move always on your belly."

Lloyd complained, "We don't have to do this in mud, do we?"

Sergeant Lavign rolled his eyes and flung out his arms. "But of course! Especially in zee mud! You will adore mud. Zee mud she save your life."

It did.

A few of us, anyway.

Chapter 17

Gondrecourt -- 1917

When the 16th Infantry tried to locate Pancho Villa in Mexico, we marched standing tall.

If we thought the Villaistas were hiding on the next hill, we would spread four or five yards apart, but we kept walking, upright, rifles at port arms.

After we in Second Platoon demonstrated this to Sergeant Lavign, he rolled his eyes.

"My friends this is merde. You mus' not walk this way against the Boche. Not ever! For you soon will be dead! All of you. Many of my comrades died so."

"So how the hell do we advance against the enemy?"

Pointing first right and then left, he said, "You mus' be like a target in, how do you say it, the arcade – zee shooting arcade at carnival. *Vous devez apparaître et puis disparaître.*"

Adamczak translated. "The sergeant said you must appear and disappear."

"Oui!" Reaching out to point opposite ways, he said, "You! Pop up here. Then fall! And you! Pop over there! Then drop! Always present different target! Jump up, run three steps. Drop! Then crawl."

I got his point and tried to explain.

"Make a quick rush, and then disappear while somebody else pops up over there and does the same. The idea is to divide their fire. You jump up and then take cover before the gunner can shift his sights to you. Get it?"

"Yeah, Sarge, we get it. But what if le bad, bad Boches have more than one machinegun aimed at you?"

After a brief chat, Adamczak said, "Sergeant Lavign says the Boche always have several machineguns aimed at you so you've got to act fast and keep firing your Chauchats at them."

"Your what?"

# # #

The Blue Devils said the weapon helping them maneuver against German positions was the Chauchat, a light single-man machinegun.

They said they used the gun on both flanks of an advancing squad to fire bursts at German trenches and machinegun positions. They said this rapid fire supposedly forced the Huns to duck while riflemen could make short dashes to get within grenade-throwing range.

Sounded great.

Later we found German machinegun teams almost never ducked.

We also discovered that the Chauchat was very awkward to use and, literally half the time, it jammed.

In my book, it was a worthless piece of crap.

But, and I never found out why, the U.S. Army wouldn't have anything to do with England's much more reliable Lewis gun. Oh, the U.S. Navy used the Lewis. But not the damned Army.

After our introduction to the Chauchat – more or less pronounced *Show-shah* — I spent an hour with Captain Bowcher, company commander, complaining about its four big flaws.

He was impressed and took me to Major Akree, the battalion exec, to describe our concerns.

"Sergeant, I'm busy," the major said, "so make it quick." I took a deep breath.

"Sir, the more I hear from the Blue Devils about what we will face in combat, the more I worry about this weapon – or this bicycle tubing that's supposed to be a weapon."

Giving me a grim look, the major said, "Sergeant, we're told the Chauchat is reliable but the captain says you have a case. So make it. Quick!"

"Well, sir, first of all, the gun's extractor is *very* reliable. We rely on it to break after we fire anywhere from ten to forty rounds. That leaves an expended shell stuck in the chamber and she no longer will fire.

"So right there in the middle of a firefight, the poor bastard gunner has to field strip the thing to try to fit in a new bolt.

"Second, the sides of the gun's 20-round magazine are wide open so, at a glance, the gunner can tell how many rounds he's got left. But those openings also reliably allow mud, dust, cow crap, twigs and pebbles in among the cartridges.

"Those objects reliably jam the feed so that she no longer fires. Same deal for the gunner … not to mention any comrades who depend on his fire power

"Third, sir, we can rely on the bicycle factory – literally, yes sir, the bicycle factory that manufactures the Chauchat -- to get the chamber dimensions wrong for .30-06 ammo, so we can rely on her not to fire at all."

"Very well, that's enough, sergeant," the major said with an icy glare. Now do you think you can just ease up on the heavy sarcasm, and just tell me the rest straight."

"Okay, sir. My apologies. But what really worries us -- and the Blue Devils themselves tell us this is the case -- the damn gun jams from one cause or another after about three hundred rounds.

"Using .30-06, sir, it often jams before we fire sixty rounds.

"Lastly, sir, the bipod legs are so long that shooting prone forces you so high above ground that you make a great target."

The major looked at our sample Chauchat. "Ugly damned thing, isn't it? And it looks awkward. It's as long as the Springfield…"

I interrupted, "Actually a few inches longer, sir."

"I was about to say, sergeant, it looks very cumbersome with the left hand grip only six inches in front of the pistol grip."

"Yessir," I said. "It's very difficult to control. In my opinion sir, it's a piece of crap."

"Yes, sergeant, I sensed that. Even so, being able to fire fifty rounds at a German machinegun crew is better than single shots from your bolt action rifle.

"I'll relay your story to Colonel Wilkins and ask him to pass up the word to regimental HQ and on to AEF. But I'm afraid for now we're stuck with it.

"Just be sure to reject any Chauchat that won't chamber our ammo. Make do with the rest."

I tried not to grit my teeth. "Yessir."

Chapter 18

Gondrecourt -- 1917

"Sarge, they told us we'd train for six weeks before going into the line. We landed in June and it's almost September. What's the hold-up?"

"Hey, what's your rush, Blackie? I'd rather we both know what we're doing before we tackle the Fritzes."

Blackwell and I and the rest of the squad were down in our dummy trench hacking with short-handled shovels to chop out a new firing step.

See, the trench itself averaged ten to twelve feet deep. But on the side facing the enemy was a crumbly ledge – the firing step – about five and a half feet from the top of the trench. Men stood on the step to fire rifles or machineguns at the Huns. Heavy rain had washed away much of the old step.

"We know what we're doing,' Flannery said. "It's all these 'cruits like Blackie who are so damned dumb about everything."

I understood Flannery's frustration. We'd been doing a lot of hand-holding with the draftees. Most of them were eager to capture Berlin, but they bitched constantly and always asked "Why?"

"Why've we only had one mail call, Sarge?"

"Sarge, why don't they pay us?"

"Sarge, why won't you let us go into town and get some of that van blonk?"

"Sarge, why do they keep feeding us this gawdawful monkey meat?" It was a canned meat – and a slimy insult to French cooking. When the Blue Devils saw it in our mess kits they grimaced in sympathy.

Otherwise, Uncle Sam fed us – breakfast, lunch and dinner -- corned beef or canned salmon, cornmeal mush and all the coffee you could drink.

Sometimes the coffee actually was hot.

Today the question came from Fothergill, the platoon loner, wondering why we were spending so much time and effort repairing a dummy front-line trench. "S-s-s-sarge, why do we have t-t-t-t-to weave together all these thousands of sticks?"

"Because, young trooper, that weave forms kind of a retaining blanket. It supports the trench walls and keeps them from collapsing in on us. You don't want to be buried alive, do you?"

"Hell, back to home," Bright said, "they used stone or concrete."

"Yeah, smart ass?" I said in exasperation. "And did you notice we don't have stone or cement here? There's none in the trenches up at the front, either. And if you ask why I'll kick your butt right out of this trench."

We at least had help from new engineer units who rotated in and out of our area apparently learning how to dig trenches.

The last engineering company even installed pumps to keep ground water from rising above the duckboards on the trench floor. Theoretically, they also would keep dugouts dry.

The last group of engineers also developed some chemical latrines that held down on the stench. We applauded their work by singing a short ballad Adamczak composed:

> *Grab your spades by the ears,*
> *You are sanitation engineers.*
> *Lay 'em big or lay 'em small*
> *You will cover up them all,*
> *You're our sanitation engineers.*

Pretending to feel insulted, the engineers scowled and cussed at us. When they left for the day, however, we noticed they marched in step while singing the tune lustily.

# # #

The toughest training focused on stealth night approaches to mock German positions manned by the very alert Blue Devils.

Major Creek, back from a special school, gave us the low-down on nighttime Australian tactics.

"Men, when outside your trench do not stand! And don't even think of climbing over barbed wire. Try it and you're a corpse hanging in the wire for all to see.

"You dare not even crawl on all fours. You snake along, flat on your belly. Using wire cutters, you cut paths through the base of barbed wire tangles.

"You cut a passage at least two feet wide and you bend the cut ends upward at least eighteen inches to get clearance. When you wiggle through that gap, keep your head down. You don't want the noise of barbed wire scraping your helmet. That's a sound that alerts them.

"Another alert is what the Aussies call the Fritz Alarm. The Germans string tin cans containing pebbles or shell casings along the barbed wire. If you jiggle one even a little, it rattles and brings their gunners wide awake … which brings a burst of bullets in your direction."

The new men looked at each other, eyes wide.

"On raids, leave your rifles behind. Take pistols – a Colt .45 automatic if you're lucky. Otherwise carry a .45 revolver. Eight shots in the one, six in t'other. Either one can knock a grizzly flat.

"But I want to stress that you must not depend on the pistol. Not at first, anyway.

"Each man is to tote at least three Mills grenades. That's what surprises, kills or at least stuns the enemy … gives you time to take prisoners or at least to yank unit badges off their uniforms."

"Sir, you mean we go right down into their trenches?"

"Maybe, Simpkins. Depends upon your assigned position. Somebody must get into their dugouts which is where you need your secondary weapon.

"It can be this," he said, holding a two-foot club studded with wicked-looking spikes. "Or, you can take one of those little shovels. They're sharp enough to slice through a face or an arm."

Holding up the club again, "Bash the Boche. Either face or shoulder. That shocks the biggest of them. Stops 'em cold. Even if you only manage to slam those big helmets with it, it's going to give your opposite number a hell of a headache."

Major Creek told us some Aussies started carrying razor-sharp bayonets to cut sentries' throats. His words caused nervous swallows among his listeners.

"You don't like the idea slicing someone's gullet?" he said. "Well, men it's a fairly quiet kill. Just as certain as a bullet or shrapnel. By the way, men, German raiders often slit the throats of dozing sentries.

"Germans also specialize in counterattacks. So snatch your Hun prisoners or Hun papers -- whatever you're after – and get back to your lines fast! Because the Huns come after you like angry hornets.

"Now look, don't fret about this! Before we raid a trench, we'll scout the ground. And we'll take you through rehearsals so everybody knows exactly what to do."

He turned to leave, stopped and faced us again.

"One more thing, men. Everybody in this outfit will draw sentry duty at one time or another. You'd better damned well not doze off. Stay *very* alert and *very* wide awake because, if you snooze, two enemies are out to kill you."

"Two enemies, sir?"

"Yep. First the Germans and then an American firing squad."

Afterwards Rozanov said, "Damn, Major Creek was pretty grim about sleeping sentries, wasn't he?"

"Damn right he was," I said. "You better be, too. As far as command and military law is concerned, a sleeping sentry is a German ally. Think about it!"

# # #

Fothergill came to me asking for a second gas mask.

"What's wrong with yours?"

"Nothing, S-s-s-s-sergeant. I want it for my cat."

"For your *cat*? General Pershing issued you a cat?"

I learned Fothergill had paid the price in bites and scratches to domesticate a barn kitten. Now it rode contentedly inside his gas mask carrier. He fretted that, once on line, the critter wouldn't survive a gas attack.

"Hell, Fothergill, a nosebag can't save it. It couldn't get that teeny mouth over the port even it knew enough to do it. And you couldn't pinch its little nostrils shut."

He explained he would seal the fluffball inside the mask. "That would work, wouldn't it?"

"Look, I doubt it. When we move to the line you best leave the little guy here."

He gave me a sullen look and walked away.

Chapter 19

On The Line -- 1917

It was a dead quiet midnight when we shuffled along the zig-zag angles of our first front line trench … after traversing the zig-zag approaches to the front line.

Wilson whispered, "Jesus, it stinks to high heaven down here!"

Simpkins whispered back, "If you don't like it, Sam, try putting on your gaspirator."

Both men cackled. We drilled with gas masks most of the morning. In afternoon, we tried playing football while wearing the devices, sheer damned misery. Worse than mask baseball.

I snapped. "Shut your holes, both of you!"

Our orders were to keep quiet so the Germans a hundred yards away wouldn't hear us taking over the trenches from a Moroccan regiment. We'd prefer the squareheads not be aware of us at least until we got to know our surroundings.

As we threaded along the darkened trench my fevered imagination amplified every rifle butt clanking against a bayonet scabbard or a canteen. Helmets clinked against each other. Every boot toe thudded against a jutting duckboard plank. The noise had me swearing under my breath.

We had the honor – so our colonel put it -- of being the army's first regiment to face Germans in the Western Front.

The distinction impressed none of us.

But the numbing cold did. So did the overpowering stench.

The Poilu sergeant guiding us gave a soft chuckle. "Oh, the stink, eh? *Tres formidable!* Our gift for you Teddies. Three very dead Boche. We buried but, of course, artillery goes 'poof'" – he demonstrated by steepling his fingers upward – "and return them to our world."

"And to our noses!" Wilson said. "Wonderful!"

"You should thank God for this cold," the Frenchman said. "In summer, *l'odeur is incroyable*."

"Oh, great. That means it can get worse?"

"*Wilson!* For God's sake, will keep a still tongue in your head?"

Our guide pulled back the blanket cloaking the entrance of a big dug-out carved deep into the trench walls. Lieutenant DuPont, our eager new CO, shined his flashlight inside on the posts supporting its timber ceiling.

"Not exactly the Ritz," he said, "but looks solid enough. Does it stand up to shelling?"

The poilu shrugged. "Who knows? This is one *bon secteur.* How you say, a quiet one? Very little artillery."

The lieutenant snorted. "Well I guess we'll find out, won't we? Okay, this is platoon HQ. Too bad we can't install some kind of heater in here."

"Right, sir," I said. "Be nice to have a fireplace with a roaring blaze."

The dugout's earth walls had four narrow shelves carved to accommodate sleepers.

Leaning closed to me, Beason asked, "It's November first and we're still in summer uniforms. Any idea why they ain't sent us winter gear?"

The lieutenant answered for me.

"Beason, it beats the hell out of me and Sergeant Coleman both! Why don't you ask General Pershing? Meanwhile, do what all the rest of us are doing. Drape your blanket over your shoulders and hug it to your body."

"Yessir. Sorry, sir!" Beason backed from the dug-out just as somebody else outside stamped his freezing feet on the duck boards.

"Dammit, Sergeant," Lieutenant Dupont said, "can't you keep your men quiet? They sound like a small elephant herd. I know they're cold. I'm cold! All God's chillun is cold. But we've no choice. We just have to endure it."

"Yessir!" I backed from the dugout and began grabbing arms and collars. In what I hoped were vicious whispers, I said, "Are you dumb bastards actually *inviting* the Boche to attack us? Don't you remember them telling us about the *Stosstruppen*?"

"The what?"

"You idiot! The Germans have special trained trench-raiding troops? Remember?"

"Oh, yeah!"

"Yeah. So shut the fuck up and keep quiet!"

# # #

Our little fraction of the Western Front stayed calm through the night and all the next day.

The Moroccans left two periscopes in First Platoon's section of the trench. The view through them was disappointing.

"Your turn," I told Flannery.

After a few minutes he said, "All I can make out are thousands of pillows, rusty barbed wire, weeds and several hacked-up trees."

Peering through the other scope, Sergeant Major Owens said, "Those pillows are sandbags, private."

After a moment he added, you can tell there ain't been much artillery fire here lately. Sandbags are pretty much intact. Grass and weeds have overgrown the shell holes."

"I can't see the Hun trenches at all," Flannery said.

Owens said, "The sandbags mark their trenches. Did you think the Heinies just put them there for fun?"

Herb Liddle, one of our draftees, asked, "Hell, how do we even know the Fritzes are there at all?"

Still at the periscope, Sergeant Owens said, "Trust me, somebody's there. You can see the smoke from those wheeled cooking stoves they have."

He backed from the periscope. "Of course, if you don't believe me, climb up here beside me on the firing step and poke your head into view. When some sniper Mausers your noggin you'll know the Germans are there."

"Thanks, Sar-major. I'll take your word for it."

By late afternoon, the faint sunlight warmed us a bit and boredom set in. After cleaning our rifles and the Chauchats and sharpening bayonets, the troops had little to do but doze or play cards and try to ignore the smell.

Save for an occasional whump-thump far in the distance, you wouldn't know a war was underway… except that we dare not climb up from our trench into the open.

 Not long after dark, two new men fired their Enfields into no man's land.

"What the hell are you shooting at?"

"Sarge, I was certain I heard somethin' moving out there," Guardino said. "Maybe an infiltrator."

"So you fired your rifle at a noise. At least you're not sleeping. Likely a rat. The French say they're thick in no-man's land." At that instant, a burst of German machinegun fire lashed overhead. "Gee, Guardino, sounds to me like you woke 'em up over there."

"Yeah, I guess."

Two flares popped up from the German lines.

Swaying under their little parachutes, the light from the flares cast moving shadows in our trench. The Germans fired a few more bursts, whipping tracers above us.

"Hey, guys!" said Converse, our felon, "you notice how them bullets crack when they go over?"

"Yeah, Converse, don't you know what that means?"

"What, Sarge?"

"It means those bullets are passing less than a foot above your thick skull."

In the flare light, Converse's eyes grew enormous. "Are you ragging me, Sarge?"

"Nope. Gospel truth. Keep your head down and stay wide awake."

Converse was one of a small group of prison inmates whom the regiment had welcomed unenthusiastically.

The cons were part of some crazy social experiment to see if bank robbers, burglars and sneak thieves could rehabilitate by serving their country.

For sure, they could march and shoot. They also were adept at stealing, sowing discord and starting fights.

Chapter 20

Hun Attack -- 1917

At midnight, hoping to sleep a bit, I wrapped my blanket around me and crawled into one of the dug-out's shelves.

Loose dirt trickled into my left ear.

I called to the guy tucking into a shelf on the other side of the dug-out. "Hey, Reeves! If you're smart you'll cover your ear with your blanket or helmet. Otherwise you get an ear full of French soil!"

He didn't answer so I mentally shrugged and tried to sleep. A runner was to wake me at 0600 so I could make the rounds and check that B Company's sentries were alert.

The Heinies got us up early.

Just about 0500, a German artillery round slammed into the earth overhead, dropping a five or six pound clump of dirt onto my covered head. The blast also sucked the air from my lungs so I was gasping as shrapnel from the next shell shredded our dug-out's entry curtain.

Stumbling from the dugout, I blew my whistle as hard as I could and drew my revolver, I bellowed, "First Platoon! Stand to! Stand to! Huns are attacking."

I doubt anybody heard me or my little whistle but they had to be awake thanks to the heavy shell fire blasting to our rear and right and left. The Limies and French had warned us about the box barrage, artillery fire to block reserves from coming to our aid.

During a pause in the shelling I heard a hollow *thonk* -- a mortar being fired. After it came a faint whine and several more *thonks*. More mortars.

A row of crimson doughnuts crashed into brief life just behind our trench. With gut-quaking blasts, two others landed fifty feet away inside our trench cloaking us in dust and smoke.

Despite the explosions, my ears caught voices and yells. At least some of our men were up and alert.

Then at the crest of the trench above me someone shouted, *"Unten, dann rechts!"* Down, to the right!

Four bodies slid feet-first into our trench, the closest landed maybe two feet away. I fired my Colt into his chest, slamming him into his nearest companion. Both collapsed.

Adamczak leaned from a dugout and cut down the other two Huns with a chugging burst from his Chauchat.

Maybe the four Germans were just a flank guard. No other Fritzes invaded our section of the trench. Meanwhile, other First Platoon men emerged with rifles and bayonets from their dug-outs ready to fight.

Through the barrage, we heard shooting to our left beyond the next trench angle. More explosions, grenades, flashed and boomed over in Second Platoon's area.

"That's where the bastards are attacking. Adamczak, come on!"

"With you, Sarge!"

Ulrich, First Platoon's other Chauchat gunner, appeared behind Adamczak.

"Ulrich, you stay here and nail any more Huns who show up! Simpkins, Beason and Wasserman! With me!" The trio had their rifles, bayonets fixed.

As we turned the trench's angle, artillery flashes gave us flickering views of several figures clambering up the trench wall. The German raid already was ending. They were headed back to cross no-man's land.

We ducked as four more blasts erupted practically in our faces. Shrapnel whizzed and Beason yelped. Grenades again, covering the German retreat.

All of us fired at the Fritzes now fleeing from the crest of the trench. Aiming was impossible in the darkness. We couldn't see whether we hurt anyone.

Following the raiders, the six of us climbed to the firing step. Simpkins, Wasserman and Beason began shooting with their rifles at the vague shapes retreating toward the German lines.

Adamzcak and Ulrich fired quick bursts. Adamczak's gun quit on the fourth burst. He raged, "Goddamn useless piece of crap!" He tried to yank out the magazine. It wouldn't budge.

"Maybe it's the damned extractor not the mag," Ulrich suggested. Then his Chauchat quit. "Awwww, Jesus!"

That's when machineguns in the German trenches began firing toward us.

"Come on men, get down," I said. "No sense getting shot when we can't see to shoot them and our guns don't work.

"Ulrich, what the hell are you doing here? I told you to stay behind to bump off any other Germans."

"Sarge, no Heinies never showed up. 'Sides, I was getting lonely."

"If you disobey any more orders, by God, I'm going to have your guts for a necktie."

"Yeah, okay Sarge."

"But thanks for showing up to help."

"Yeah, okay Sarge."

Chapter 21

Aftermath – 1917

Dawn showed Second Platoon's section of trench to be a gory mess. Clots of mud thrown up by grenades dotted the faces of the dead and wounded.

The night's survivors seemed to be in shock, stumbling about aimlessly.

I did what sergeants always must. I got their brains back in gear by damning them with curt, ruthless orders.

"You sorry sons-a-bitches! Look at here!. I have lost all respect for Private Evans because he let the Bosche slit his throat clear to the bone!

"And the rest of you! Standing around with your brains in neutral and your thumbs up your butt when wounded buddies need help. Get busy!

"First step, stop their bleeding! Then carry them to the aid station.

"Now get cracking!"

Simpkins, Beason, Wasserman and I hoisted Converse onto a stretcher and headed down the communication trench to the aid station. When we returned, we found Flannery dealing with a man's huge leg wound.

Flannery was pale. "Good God," he whispered, "I never knew a man had so much blood in him."

"Probably bout the same as in a full grown hog," I said brutally.

Two other wounded men gave screams about as shrill as a butchered hog as they were manhandled onto stretchers.

"You boys," I yelled, "keep these sights and sounds in mind next time you have sentry duty."

Wasserman swallowed, "Right, sarge."

Second Platoon's senior corporal had to call roll because the Germans had captured his sergeant. The roll call showed that the raiders made off with ten other members of the platoon as well.

I reported the butcher's bill to Lieutenant Dupont.

"The Huns killed three of our men, sir, two by gunfire, the third by slitting his throat. Fifteen other men are wounded. Five look pretty serious, mainly from grenades."

"Dammit, sergeant, do you have anything good to report?"

"Well, a bit, sir. To the good, we nailed seven squareheads. In First Platoon, we got lucky and killed four and second Platoon ventilated three of the bastards."

"Yeah, fine," the lieutenant said, "but what a Goddamned debacle. It's a German victory. No two ways about it. In ten minutes, they knocked First platoon down to a third of its strength. Presumably that man with his throat cut was a sentry taken unawares."

"Looks that way," I said. "He could have been sound asleep at his post. I'd say he's an object lesson for the other sentries from now on."

I didn't talk about it, but something about the dead rattled me … including the two Germans I shot.

Their eyes.

At my family's funeral way back in Michigan City, the undertaker made sure that Mom, Dad and Sis looked peacefully asleep.

The eyes of most of the dead in our trench this morning, however, were half-open. Most of them looked half awake and about to sit up.

None moved, of course.

On looking closer, you'd see their eyeballs had dried, taking away the shine or gleam or whatever you call it in the eyes of living human beings.

I shuddered and not because of the cold.

The French and the British armies employed either civilians or service troops to carry away their wounded and bury their dead.

Not the AEF.

Right down at the squad level, our men got the detail of carrying off their own wounded and also burying their own dead comrades.

It was rotten for morale.

On this one occasion, it at least was some comfort that the French politely took away the remains of the three dead Americans.

They buried the three men that same morning in a ceremony near a small town, Bathelemont, just behind our lines.

# # #

None of us was aware of the French gesture at the time we returned from Second Platoon's bloody trench to First Platoon's.

Adamczak pointed at the Germans' bodies and said, "Well, at least the raid cost them more dead than us."

Captain Bowcher, who walked with us said, "Damned poor consolation when they dragged eleven of our boys back with them. Prisoners."

"What I can't figure," Beason mused, "is how they got to our trench so fast. I mean what with the wire tangles and all out in no man's land."

"Probably Bangalore torpedoes," the captain said.

"What's that, sir?"

"It's a long explosive tube," he explained. "What you do is shove it under the wire. Light it, duck and 'boom!' If it's placed right, it can open a clear avenue right through the wire."

"We got any of those torpedo things, Cap'n?"

"Not yet."

Beason interrupted us.

"Would you look at this? Guess I got hit during the night."

Opening his bloodied shirt, he plucked a tiny steel splinter from the skin of his breastbone. It had ripped through his gas mask and its carrier.

"So I'm wounded, eh?"

"No, Beason," I said. "Your gas mask is wounded. You'd best get to Supply for a new one."

"Well, shit!" Blackwell said. "When you consider that the Germans have our men, now they'll know everything about us. They'll torture our men until they confess everything."

"I don't know about that," Simpkins said. "If they captured me, by God, I'd tell them *alllll* about the 16th so they'd know they're facing the varsity team now. With us Yanks in the war it's just a question of time. It's all going downhill for them."

"Not unless we fight a hell of a lot smarter than we did last night," I said.

"Damn right," the captain said.

"Look, since First Platoon lost its sergeant," he went on, "it needs some stiffening. So First Sergeant Coleman, take over until we get a seasoned replacement."

Lieutenant Dupont asked, "In addition to his regular duties, sir?"

"For now, just Second Platoon."

"Sergeant," the captain added, "the Seconds' morale is shot. I'd like you to go and have a talk with them. I'm sure they'll take it better from you than they would from an officer."

Chapter 22

Recovering – 1917

I returned to my bunker to clean up before going back to Second Platoon.

It surprised me to see Reeves huddled and shivering in front of our little alcohol stove, blanket still over his shoulders.

He looked up at me, lips trembling "Are they gone yet?"

"Who?"

"The Germans."

"Hell yes! We killed seven of them. I did in two of them right in front of this dugout. One shot! Wait! That was two, three hours ago. Reeves, did you stay in here the whole time?"

"Yes."

"You stayed here safe in this bunker throughout our fight?"

He ducked his head.

"Reeves, are you a goddam coward?"

"I didn't think so until last night, Sarge. But …guess I was scared."

"You *guess* you were scared?"

He nodded, tears welling up in his eyes.

I stared in disbelief. "Shit, Reeves, everybody was scared! I sure as hell was! You let us down -- your buddies! You know you could be court-martialed and shot for this? More likely they'd send you to Fort Leavenworth for life."

"Oh, God, Sarge, don't let that happen! Please, I beg you." Now he was bawling like a child. "My family couldn't take it," he wailed. "It'd destroy our reputation. Just shoot me right now and get it over with."

"Shoot you? Bullshit, I can't do that! I won't! I'll march you to the CO and he'll turn you over to the provost marshal for a general court martial."

"Please don't do that, Sarge. I couldn't take it. I just couldn't!"

Flannery entered the dug-out behind me. "I overheard that!" Imitating a small child's whine he said, "I can't take it! I just can't!

"Reeves," he said, "you sniveling little rat bastard. Look at the blood on my hands! I just finished trying to save Smitty's left leg which took most of a grenade blast. Jesus, you're sickening."

Flannery turned to me. "Sarge, what are you gonna do with him?"

"I don't know. Turn him over to Lieutenant DuPont, I guess."

"I've got a better idea," Flannery said. "Don't do anything. Just leave the worthless little shit right here. The word will get around. He'll either shoot himself or one of the guys will do it for him."

It was tempting. The men would ostracize him. Instead of a thousand deaths, this coward would suffer ten thousand deaths. But it also would poison the company's morale just as we were trying to rebuild it.

"Guess not," I said. "Then we'd both be a party to a murder."

"Come on, Reeves," I said. "We're going to the CO's dugout."

"No! I won't do it!"

"Okay, then you can bawl like a baby while Flannery and I drag you."

We dragged him. He bawled all the way.

The next day, MPs took him to a prison stockade near headquarters at Chaumont.

# # #

During that miserable event, the French were paying a special tribute to our Second Platoon casualties.

Major Creek represented the 16th Infantry at the burial ceremony in Bathelemont. He told us a French general conducted it.

"He gave a very moving little speech," he said. "He pledged that they would establish a permanent monument to the first three Americans to die in combat. He thanked them in the name of France."

When we rotated out of the line two weeks later, we saw three elderly workers putting the finishing touches on a low dark marble tomb.

Two flagpoles surmounted the tomb, one flying the French tricolor the other the stars and stripes. The workers also were laying pavers around the tomb.

Adamzcak said the workers told him the French government planned to erect a giant headstone with a bronze plaque.

Chapter 23

Freezing – 1917-18

It seemed to help Second Platoon's hang-dog survivors when I explained that they really hadn't suffered a defeat.

"Men, this was just a raid, not a real battle! I grant you, the Fritzes caught us napping and accomplished their mission."

Heads hung dejectedly at that remark.

Then I shouted, "BUT did you boys notice that they didn't hang around so much as one second to gloat or to keep this little piece of America?

"Nossir! They scampered away just as fast as their stumpy little legs could carry them. The squareheads knew that if they didn't skedaddle, you'd slaughter them all."

More nodding and now some grins.

"We'll take some steps, men, to make sure this kind of thing don't happen again without them getting a very, very bloody nose. For one thing, the regiment's machinegun battalion will attach a permanent Hotchkiss to us – along with its crew and lots of ammo. The Heinies ain't gonna sneak up on us with that thing around, are they?"

I won't say Second Platoon actually cheered, but they did brighten up a bit.

Yes, my little speech was pure bullshit. Both Lieutenant DuPont and I agreed on that as he helped me compose the message. We just didn't want the survivors spreading gloom or a sense of defeat to the rest of the company.

As it was, the 16th Regiment already had enough to worry about aside from what occurred during the raid.

Now, none of this was official.

But the rumor mill had circulated a scary story that the whole damned French Army had mutinied.

I went so far as to ask Major Creek about the tale. He put on a pretty convincing act in denying it. He pretended to be angry that I'd dare ask such a question about our allies and host country.

So I figured the answer actually was "yes."

Our own Frog buddies, the *Chasseurs* and the Moroccans indirectly seemed to verify the rumor because they seemed very downcast and dejected.

When I asked Sergeant Lavign about mutiny, the tough little Frenchman blustered. "That talk is *merde*! I tell you, Yankee, I and my *soldats* fight like hell to defend France. You say otherwise, I smash your face!"

"Whoa, Sargent! Okay! Ease up, please! No offense!"

Once I got him calmed down, Lavign explained that the bulk of French soldiers made it clear from now on they'd refuse to march like sheep into sacrificial attacks.

As time went on, we heard more and more that the straw breaking French troops' morale was an abortive French offensive while we still were in Mexico.

The attack failed miserably during its first hours.

But instead of calling it off, their commander – a General named Neville -- ordered the assault to continue against massed German artillery and machine guns. It went on for days, a one-sided slaughter killing tens of thousands of French troops to no purpose whatever.

The Frog government sacked the general. Supposedly some reforms were underway in the French army. But that word "mutiny" still made a hell of a scary impression.

Meanwhile, we Yanks were struggling with a problem all our own.

As autumn deepened into winter – and it was one of Europe's coldest, hardest winters in decades -- we were freezing. Most of us still were in summer uniforms. So our teeth chattered non-stop, our lips were blue and fingers and toes felt permanently frozen.

Some of our college men said it was Valley Forge all over again, only this time in northeast France instead of Pennsylvania. "At least, we aren't starving," Adamczak said, "not like George Washington's boys back in 1777-78."

"Oh hell no," Flannery groused. "We have great food -- canned salmon, corned beef and cornmeal mush. It gets through to us even if it's usually was frozen rock-solid."

"Yep," Adamczak grinned. "You always can thaw that mush by holding a block of it in your armpit. And you know that such a practice makes life tough for your lice."

Headquarters assured us that they requisitioned winter gear clear back in July. But only a trickle of the clothing ever arrived. Reportedly it was a lack of shipping that left our brown woolens piled up in New York and New Jersey harbor warehouses.

Hugging his blanket to his chest, Wasserman said, "You know what this means, don't you? It'll be a nice hot July day when all those heavy clothes get delivered to the docks at St. Nazaire."

He was wrong.

They actually arrived in June.

We suspected that the few greatcoats, boots and gloves that made it to France this year wound up warming staff officers at Chaumont, AEF's headquarters.

One day I got a bit hot under the collar when I spotted General Pershing talking with General Bullard, our division commander.

Bullard looked chilly in an ordinary dress jacket complete with Sam Browne belt. But a thick greatcoat with a turned-up collar cloaked the AEF commander from neck to ankles.

The biggest concern for everybody, however, was that Russia had quit the war.

I think that news deeply worried everyone from the top allied commanders down to the truck drivers and stretcher-bearers.

Even the dullest private probably figured Ludendorff and Hindenburg were routing troop trains from the Eastern Front to France.

Those trains would carry dozens of full divisions of veteran German troops into the trenches facing us and our allies … hundreds of thousands of tough Fritzes along with their rifles, machineguns and artillery.

This in turn meant that come spring, we – Yanks, French and British – would be the target of an enormous German offensive.

Unfortunately, only six divisions of Americans so far had arrived in France.

Chapter 24
On Defense – 1917-18

"Sir, I get the impression that our allies don't think too much of us as fighting men."

Captain Bowcher chuckled. He just returned from touring a group of British staff officers through our new location near Ansauville.

"Yes," the captain said. "Kind of a looking-down-your-nose attitude. Of course maybe that's because we're in a Frog sector.

"Anyhow, they also gave the impression that our boys were a little too casual in officers' presence. They expected lads on watch in the trenches to slam to attention and give perfect salutes. Shocking lack of discipline, old boy."

I snorted. "Too bad they weren't here three nights ago when the local Bosche tried to raid us."

Our regiment moved into this section of the front a week back, this time making no attempt to disguise our arrival.

Thanks to a thaw, the trenches were an odorous, sloppy mess. Snow melt submerged some of our duckboard walkway and flooded the latrines. On a scale of ten, the smell was a solid eighteen.

But my main complaint – aside from hearing everybody else's grousing – is that you couldn't get clean. Place a palm for balance against the muddy face of the trench and a minute later unconsciously scratch ear or nose. By the afternoon, only your eyes are not crusted with filth.

At full darkness each night, every platoon sent two two-man listening posts slithering out in front of our lines. The first night, I hovered to make sure Sergeant DeVries gave the correct instructions.

"Look, your job in the outpost ain't to fight the squareheads but to alert us. We'll do the fighting.

"So find yourselves a nice deep hole fifty yards out front of our trench. Once you get there stay low, stay quiet, keep each other awake, and keep your ears open and your eyes peeled.

"Now for God's sake, no smoking! The Fritzes will spot you and kill you. Then because *you* doped off, *we* would get it in the neck! Besides, it would really set off the old man's temper."

"What do you mean, Sarge?"

"The cap'n would have to take time away from his Scotch to write one of those I-regret-to-inform-you letter to your folks back home. That's why."

As the chuckles died down, the sergeant added, "Now look, when you spot moving Huns, let us know. You can throw a grenade into the Fritzes. Or you can fire two shots with your pistol – but point it into the muck so's they can't see the muzzle flash.

"Main thing is that you alert us. Then protect your own ass."

# # #

On the third night, one outpost tossed a grenade. The blast alerted us. So did the screams from a wounded German. We were ready, half of us on standby.

The grenade disrupted the attack plan.

While maybe 50 or so Germans raced toward our trench, perhaps an equal number became confused and either did nothing or started to retreat.

We in the trenches opened up on the attackers with rifles and machineguns. The noise was horrendous even if, due to the difficulty of aiming in darkness, we didn't hit all that many Huns.

A knot of perhaps 40 Heinies made it to our line, lobbing stick grenades into the trench. After the explosions, they came sliding down into our position.

Then the rest of us, our little platoon reserve, threw our own grenades at the Huns. I counted at least five blasts, most of them close to the Germans.

They were still stunned when we charged at them through the smoke. It became a free-for-all. The sounds reminded me of football … snarls, thuds, grunts, yells, curses, clanks and a few screams.

I carried my revolver but also wielded a spiked medieval-looking bludgeon. I backhanded it against the side of a German's face, it banged his helmet sideways as he yelled and dropped. Beside me, Wasserman chopped a short-handled shovel through the throat of a big Heinie sergeant. The blood splashed us all.

In the confusing dark, it looked as if several Germans clustered near a dugout entrance. Orange muzzle flashes showed they were shooting pistols. Somebody broke up the group with two short Chauchat bursts. After that, Fritzes seemed to flee every which way.

Guardino grabbed the tunic of a Fritz trying to climb from the trench. He yanked him down with a splash down onto the duckboards. "Stay there you bastard!" He viciously kicked the prisoner's crotch .

I've no idea how long the trench fight lasted. I recall a German shouting *"Raus! Zurük!"* Out! Go back!

Others raised their hands in surrender.

Somebody fired a red flare into the air. The flare must have been a signal because the Germans sent over a shower of mortars to cover their retreating troops. Two shells landed in our trench, killing four men and injuring a dozen.

At dawn, I found Lloyd and Davies. Their bodies showed how mortar shrapnel shreds human flesh.

Guardino picked up his muddy prisoner and slammed the kid against the trench wall. He bellowed into his face. "Well, what say, my *tedesco amico*? Can us Americans fight, or what?"

Looking at the *feldgrau* bodies cluttering the trench floor, I just nodded. "No doubt about that. We fight!"

And now everybody – especially Germans – knew it.

Chapter 25

Attacking – June 1918

"I can't believe it! Birds are singing." No question, I heard a melodic call like a meadowlark. Just what you expect in the first days of June.

But my ears caught the song only intermittently between gasps of my breath and the crash of artillery shells.

I couldn't birdwatch because our company was racing – well, trying to race -- across a muddy, broken moonscape.

"Keep moving, dammit," I yelled. "Keep moving!"

I don't really know why I yelled. The boys moved as fast as they could pull their boots from foot-sucking muck. Maybe yelling just helped me handle my own fear.

Even so, way in the back of my mind, I still wondered where the hell the dumb birds could be present and chirping during a battle.

None was in sight as I slid down into a shell hole, splashed across its muddy pond and clambered up the far side. I saw no bird as I teetered along the narrow rim between two more shell holes. I ignored the holes' ponds -- cess pools, really, containing liquescent corpses.

If sparrows or larks *were* flying, could they dodge the falling shells of the barrage we followed? Every two minutes, our gunners advanced the shelling another hundred yards. We kept as close as possible to the line of explosions. Shrapnel scythed in the Fritzes' direction, though an occasional base plate spun backwards toward us.

For sure no bird had any place to roost. The only trees were splintered trunks bare of limbs or summertime leaves.

"Keep going!" I yelled.

We were crossing what had been a farm. *"How can they ever get a crop growing here again? How will they fill in all the shell holes?"*

Our burdens made it tough going. In addition to rifle and ammo, each man carried a big bundle of empty sandbags. Three dozen men also had lashed long-handled shovels to their packs, the steel spades jutting well above their helmets like crescen-shaped flags.

Our company was part of a battalion attack supporting our sister regiment, the 28th Infantry. We were passing the south fringe of a little burg called Cantigny. The 28th captured the town three days earlier, pushing its German occupiers onto a wooded ridge five hundred yards to the east.

The Huns counterattacked, driving the 28th out of the woods back into the town. The 28th counterattacked in turn and the battle see-sawed between town and wood. Meanwhile, German artillery reduced Cantigny to masonry dust and matchwood.

Before we left our trenches to join the attack, Lieutenant DuPont explained the maneuver.

"The 28th took heavy losses. So we need shovels and sandbags to dig a line of strong trenches that'll keep the Germans out of Cantigny and permanently penned beyond the ridge."

As he tied a spade to his own pack he added, "We have to move fast. When we get there, we gotta dig fast because the Fritzes will figure what we're about and start throwing cow pies at us."

After I passed the word to corporals and sergeants, I reported back to the lieutenant. He and Captain Bowcher emerged from their dug-out. "Are we ready?"

"Yessir," I yelled. "We're ready!"

"Okay, Sarge! Over the top." We blew our whistles and the troops climbed from the fire steps out into the open.

We were pretty well spread out, so I'd say we covered a good hundred yards before the Huns spotted us.

Once the Germans caught on, they turned at least three Maxims to chop up our ranks. Within seconds they got our range. The low-pitched *waowww* of bullets added to birdsong.

Maxim bullets kicked up mud spouts around and among us. Something clanked near me, knocking Beason flat on his back.

Wilson stooped beside him and started laughing. Beason was jarred but untouched. A German bullet punched a hole dead center in the spade tied to his pack, the impact knocking him flat. Wilson reached to help Beason who cussed as he got back to his feet.

I yelled, "Get moving! You're sheer targets right now."

My warning came too late.

Wilson's helmet clanked and flew off. Blood spewed and holes magically exploded in both their shirts. They absorbed a full burst from a Maxim, the impacts slamming them to the mud.

Wilson spasmed and was still. Beason never moved.

As we kept running, two of the Frogs' Schneider tanks came to our aid. Looking a bit like boxcars on tracks, they pitched and rolled crossing the wretched terrain. From time to time, each stopped and used its short-barrel 75 mm cannon to blast the enemy line. Their attack seemed to pulverize some German machinegun nests.

We also got help from airplanes, French Spads I think.

A group of four took turns snarling low beyond the wooded ridge, machineguns sputtering. I had the impression that they made things uncomfortable for the German artillery crews.

Maybe it was just wishful thinking on my part. But we did seem to get a brief pause in artillery fire.

Then sparks cascaded from one of the tanks -- a direct artillery hit. Smoke gushed from its sponson and the tank halted, rocking to an internal blast.

It burned, pouring thick black smoke partially screening us from Heinie gunners. The smoke also carried a strong odor of roasting meat . In ten minutes artillery crushed the other tank.

Chapter 26

Cantigny – Spring 1918

Lieutenant DuPont waved to us. "Yo, Sarge! Bring the men up here!" Using his walking staff, he pointed north to the wide-open field between Cantigny and the woods.

As we arrived, he pulled off his pack and waved his staff north and south. "Start digging along here, men. Let's get these shell holes connected into a trench."

Obviously figuring his intentions, German artillery crews began dropping shells into the earth around us.

"Look boys," the lieutenant shouted, "the Huns are helping us dig!"

As he shoved his spade into the mud, Ulrich yelled, "Bullshit, lieutenant! Those dirty bastards beyond that ridge are doing their best to kill us!"

Lieutenant DuPont yelled, "Alright. So quit yammering and start digging! Dig like crazy!"

In a way we were lucky. The muddy earth absorbed much of the blast and at least some of the shrapnel from the enemy shells.

That mud luck, however, didn't extend to our commanding officer.

A jagged piece of Krupp steel ripped through the lieutenant's torso, strewing his bloody guts ten feet beyond him. He died without a sound.

We dug frantically but at first it was a very slow, frustrating process.

"God, Sarge, this is a complete bitch of a job."

"I know!" I yelled. "*I know*! But keep digging, man! We've got to have trenches to protect us from this goddam shelling."

The problem was trying to toss about eight pounds of gooey mud stubbornly clinging to your spade while playing close heed to the rasp of arriving German artillery shells. "Hell of a deal," Simpkins said, "trying to dig the dirt while trying not to hit the dirt."

Seconds later, he failed to hit the dirt. A shell killed him and splintered his spade. The German artillery also butchered Wasserman, and Rozanov.

Yet the three dead men were a tremendous unintentional help … they were the only solid objects available against which we could thump our loaded shovels to dislodge the clinging muck.

Once we dug down two feet, the dirt was fairly dry so that we didn't need to use our half-buried comrades' bodies any longer. Now digging more quickly we still had to stop when somebody yelled. "Bosche attack!"

It was a relief to drop shovels, grab rifles, hit the dirt, and begin picking off Fritz attackers. For once we needed our firearms' long-range sights and the hours of practice on shooting ranges. We were able to see and hit our Hun targets at 300 yards.

German machinegun bullets whined overhead and pocked the dirt near us. At first it scared me shitless. But old habits instilled by months of training came to the rescue.

Cock. Aim. Shoot Five times. Push in another five-round stripper clip. Work the bolt, chambering the first round. Aim. Shoot. Cock again.

We kept it up automatically even when bullets danced among us, pitching mud and grit into our faces.

I'd call our fire withering.

Though the Fritzes bounced in and out of sight during short rushes, we knocked them down like bowling pins.

"Hey, check that!" Adamczak crowed. "Them coal-scuttle helmets don't stop a direct hit from a .30-06. That slug went right on through!"

Maybe ten minutes later we were digging again.

"Hey, Sarge," Blackie yelled. "I got a wounded man here."

"Yeah," I shouted, "bring him down here in the trench! It's safer."

Blackwell was breathless, toting Liddle in a fireman's carry. Liddle screamed as Blackwell tried to lower him gently to the trench floor.

"He's hit real bad in the shoulder Sarge." The shoulder looked like exploded gristle. Liddle's blood glistened on Blackwell's back and Liddle's contorted face was sheet white.

As we shoveled our trench deeper, more and more wounded were brought to shelter in it.

Wesley took a round through the chest and out the back. Flannery stumbled in next with a belt cinched around his left forearm.

"Lookit," he gasped angrily. "Shrapnel done it! Took off my hand neat as a surgeon. Didn't even feel it. Couldn't believe it when I saw it. I can stay and maybe help with the wounded. "

A lookout pitched backwards, face and throat blasted open with grit and pebbles hurled by another German shell. Nobody could help. At least he was unconscious and not screaming. He just gurgled and wheezed for the two minutes it took him to bleed to death.

By late afternoon, most of us were hollow-eyed and barely able to move. We not only were weary from digging but also filling and pitching the dead weight of sandbags up to crown the lip of the trench.

"Men! That ain't good enough. We need double rows of sandbags!

"A Mauser round goes right through a single bag. It takes the second bag in behind the first to stop that slug! So keep digging, keep filling, keep piling."

It was about the hardest imaginable labor.

Making it worse was the need to tread carefully between the dead, the dying and the wounded carpeting the trench floor.

"God, almighty," Guardino said. "This place is like a damned slaughter house."

"No, it's a hell of a lot worse," I said. "Butchers are merciful. Armour and Swift don't let cattle and hogs suffer. Got no choice here."

"Can't we get these men back to an aid station?"

"Not 'til full dark," I said. "The closest station is clear back in Cantigny. We tried to evacuate three of the wounded but all that open ground is a kill zone for Hun artillery, machineguns and snipers."

I knew in my gut that trying to race a stretcher while trying to dodge bullets across that jumbled three hundred yards of craters would be impossible.

All we could do was give the wounded what water we had in our canteens. They soon ran dry.

At dusk the cry went up again,

"Rifles up! Another Heinie attack."

All the shelling had cut our company's numbers down, but our rifle fire did the same to the German troops.

"Guardino," I asked as I reloaded my rifle, "are you a church-goer?"

"Hell, yeah. Since I was a kid. I say my rosary, too."

"Well, I gave it up when my family died," I said. "But right here today I thank God for all our hours on the range. I mean it for real," I fired again.

"Amen," he said.

Our Springfields, Enfields and Hotchkiss machineguns saw to it that German troops never stepped foot into Cantigny again.

More important, we showed Frogs and Tommies we could fight like devils.

Chapter 27

Cantigny – June 1918

When night fell we felt safe enough to carry the wounded to Cantigny's aid station … the empty halves of basements below two shattered cottages.

Near dawn I returned to the trench staggering because I was so whipped.

"Where've you been?" Captain Bowcher sounded angry. I was too tired to care.

"Been carrying wounded to the aid station … sir"

"Well, I've been looking for you. With Lieutenant Dupont gone I need you to take over Second Platoon."

"Jesus, Cap'n, I don't know if I can handle that right now."

"Yes you can, sergeant. It'll only be until we find another lieutenant," he said. "Besides, you ran the show most of the day yesterday."

"Oh, sir, I think I can do the work alright. It's just that I'm about to collapse. Carrying casualties is the most brutal detail I think I've ever undertaken.

"What do you mean?" he asked.

"Well, sir, to start with you got four men to a stretcher trying to find their way in the dark over badly broken ground. It's just crater on top of crater out there.

"You try your damnedest not to jar the poor bastard groaning there on the litter. But it's impossible. Even if you were on level ground in the light of day, the four of you couldn't march in step because you couldn't see each other's feet. So with every step, the litter twitches and that jostling hurts your patient.

"But, of course, it isn't level ground, sir. The men in front might be going diagonally down into one shell hole while the guys in back are climbing up the side of another.

"And your hands, Jesus!"

"Your hands? What about them?"

"Sir, the handles on most of those stretchers are splintered from being dropped or stepped on or getting soaked and then drying, or freezing and thawing.

"After about ten minutes your palms are raw and hurt like hell. You want to switch positions on the stretcher to use a different hand, but you just can't do that because you're trying to get the casualty to the doc fast as you can. Some of those wounded boys were laying in the trench all day long.

"Anyway, one guy begs to put the stretcher down. Or sometimes one guy falls and in the dark the rest go down, too, dumping the casualty into the mud. Either way, it's hell for the casualty.

"Well, an hour of that to cover three hundred yards and your bones ache such that you're ready for a night's sleep. But when you get to the aid station you find out it's all been for nothing. Your patient died somewhere on the way.

"And there's more wounded to be transported. So you go back to do it all over again. It's just plain brutal, sir. And you just pray you aren't the next one on a stretcher."

The captain cleared his throat. "Well, sergeant, from now on maybe we can see if the enemy will respect a flag of truce so that we can carry stretchers during the day."

"Tried it yesterday, sir. The fucking Fritzes wouldn't honor our white flag. Sniped two of our stretcher-bearers. I think they have orders to be as hard on us as they can. Maybe they want to see if American soldiers have the guts."

I paused.

"Anyway, out of my original squad, sir, four men are still standing. What's the company's butcher bill?"

"Donno yet, sergeant. But it'll be steep."

# # #

I should have kept my mouth shut.

Apparently the captain told battalion that maybe Germans facing us might have orders to be especially tough on American troops.

So battalion wanted to know whether our opponents could be a contingent of hard cases fresh from Russia. That seems to have been why we drew the assignment to catch a prisoner.

It made zero sense to me. An 8 mm Mauser fired by an Eastern Front veteran can't kill you one bit deader than one fired by a Fritz who's spent the war on the Western Front.

But, like Owens said, officers do the thinking and we enlisted men follow their orders.

I didn't see that I could send the boys off to do the job on their own. So I named nine of them to go, Blackwell and Guardino from my old squad plus Andy Hart and six men from First Platoon.

We departed in two elements, three First Platoon men with Blackwell and me. Andy led Guardino and the rest.

I've already described how I lost my prisoner and my friend Blackie. Thanks to all the confusion and noise, I didn't know that the other team in our raid made it home intact and with two POWs.

It was just about dawn when I heard someone yell my name from the direction of our lines.

"Max! *Max!* Are you still with us?" It sounded like Andy.

"Hell yes! I'm trapped in a hole out here!"

"Wounded?"

"Only my pride, Andy. But Blackie's dead!"

"Hang on, Max! Keep your head down. Help is on the way!"

About five minutes later, a very heavy barrage began slamming along the German trenches behind me. It forced their machine gunners to shelter in their bunkers. Then came a flash and blast to my front. I snatched a quick peek and saw a yawning gap in the wire.

I gathered my legs under me, jumped up to run and immediately fell. My legs were dead numb. So, digging in and pulling with my elbows, I hauled myself toward the gap in the wire. *Like a damned lizard, but at least I'm moving.*

By the time I got to the gap in the wire, life returned to my legs. I was able to progress on all fours.

Andy yelled, "Hurry up, Max. We've only got another minute in the barrage!"

By now I was able to do a gimpy half-gallop, just in time to slip and slide sideways into our trench.

Andy helped me to my feet. "Jesus, Max, you look like a mud pie. What took you so long to get here?"

I leaned back against the fire step and took a deep breath. "Look, just get off my back, will you? I was busy."

"Oh yeah? Busy doing what?"

"Lying low, my friend. Things were kind of dicey out there. I had no place to go. What did you do to blow that hole in the wire for me?"

"Bangalore torpedoes. Just got 'em from the Frogs. Handy as hell, eh?"

"Damn right. Now I'd better report to Bowcher. He's probably going to rip me apart because, far as I know, I'm the only survivor."

Andy shook his head. "I wouldn't worry. The Bosche were so focused on you guys, that we had no problem at all. We busted them with grenades, nabbed two of them and we all made it back. One of your people came with us."

"Andy, were your prisoners from the Russian Front?"

"Hell no! They've been in this part of the line for two years. They told us the Russian veterans are going into the trenches opposite the Tommies."

Chapter 28

Cootyville – June 1918

What was left of Company B rotated off the line, headed direct to a delousing station.

A medico of some sort, a quartermaster sergeant, met us in front of the big tent. "Where's the rest of your company?"

"This is it," I said. "We're all here."

"Hell," he said, "we're set up for a whole company, Company B. This is no more than a platoon. Where's everybody else?"

Adamzcak said, "They're either on the wire or pushing up daisies or in the hospital."

"Holy, shit," the medico muttered. Then he raised his voice.

"Well, okay, men, here's where you get rid of your cooties and seam squirrels. Peel off them uniforms! Everything! Drawers, socks and all. Throw them all in those bins beside you. Carry your shoes."

Everyone immediately began bitching. "Look, sergeant, all we need is sleep. Besides, what the hell are we going to wear?"

"The Army says you need to be deloused because otherwise you can get typhus. It can kill you. Besides, won't it be nice not to itch and scratch all the time? You'll sleep better, I guarantee.

"As far as uniforms, don't worry. Once we finish killing them lice, you'll get spanking clean uniforms. And then you can sleep all you want."

Just as we began yanking off our muddy stinking duds, Titus hissed, "Whoa! Ladies coming!"

Walking past our line were two nurses clad in starched ankle-length cone-shaped white gowns. Long pure white scarf-like head gear concealed their hair.

Seeing the nurses, most of us held garments in front of our crotches. The older nurse grinned.

"Don't worry, boys. You don't have a thing that we haven't seen before." The younger nurse didn't so much as glance up. She looked exhausted.

Once shed of our clothing, we were quite a sight. Browned faces and forearms, puckered fishbelly white everywhere else – except the red areas scratched raw because of lice.

Before we processed into the tent they gave us clippers that smelled of alcohol so we could hoe off the hair we hadn't been able to cut for a while.

Once into the tent, they practically dragged us through big tubs with khaki-colored medicinal-smelling bath water. Then we were able to soap up and rinse off in a cold shower, afterwards getting hit front and back with what felt like a pound of some white powder.

The powder made me sneeze six times in succession. "What the hell is that powder?"

"Just anti-cootie powder, Sarge. Kills what the bath don't. Now bring your boys into the next tent to draw new uniforms."

The uniforms were cleaned and pressed, but a lot of them weren't exactly new.

"Uh, I don't like this," Ulrich said. "I think I'm wearing a dead man's shirt." The uniform shirt exhibited two holes, one an oblong in the left breast pocket and the other a simple .30 caliber hole dead center between two buttons.

"Hey, Fred," Guardino said. "I wouldn't worry. You know how lightning don't never strike the same place twice?"

"Yeah, so?"

"Well, it's gotta be the same with bullets. That shirt's charmed. You can't get hit in those places."

Ulrich said, "What do you think about that, sarge?"

"Well, Fred, who's to say those are bullet holes? They could be something chewed by moth millers, you know. Like Guardino said, I wouldn't worry about it."

"I won't," Ulrich said. "Besides, I'm too tired to care one way or the other. I'm headed to the barn loft."

It took our little convoy about twenty minutes to get us back to the little French farm that was to quarter us.

The ride was rough. I had a theory that our truck's little Annamese driver steered to slam his wheels into every chuckhole. But most of the boys slept anyway.

An elderly couple watched as we painfully eased ourselves down from the trucks. The old lady wept and kept saying, "*Oh, ces pauvres enfants.*" Oh, the poor boys.

As we filed into the barn, she and her husband handed each of us an apple. I was so tired the only word coming to mind was, "Gracias." At dusk a nightmare awaked me. I picked up my apple and bit a big chunk from it. *Damn! I shoulda told them 'Merci.'*

Oddly, the nightmare wasn't about combat. It was stock yard days again. First I saw Maria holding a handkerchief to her nose, being disgusted by me, the snatcher, conveying hogs upside down to the sticker … and huge crimson gouts splashing to the kill floor.

Sitting there staring at the barn's rafters, I noticed I still held the unchewed bite of apple in my mouth. As I commenced to chew, I became aware of nightmares underway all around me.

Most of the boys writhed in their sleep. Some gasped. Others twitched, giving little cries like dogs chasing squirrels in their dreams.

As I took a second bite of the apple I hoped that's all they chased. Suddenly I fell on my side, just too whipped to stay upright. I was scared to sleep because of nightmares. But I couldn't stay awake.

This time I dreamed facing the same German trench raid again and again. Each time I tried something different to fend off the Bosche, but nothing worked.

Chapter 29

Tours – June 1918

Mulling over my nightmare's fruitless defenses against the Bosche, I dragged out my tattered copy of the Royal Army's *Hasty Fire Cover and Concealment.*

After skimming the first few page, I remembered it dealt only with squads or platoon-size actions. Not a word about how you fend off a division, let alone a whole damned German army corps.

The manual certainly didn't contain a grain of comfort or advice for everyone's growing worry about enormous masses of German troops transferring from Russia.

I groaned aloud, "There's got to be a way…"

Hart startled me. "Max, what the hell are you moaning about? You should be happy. Look, we're out of the line. We have beer. Nobody's shooting at us."

"Well, Andy, I don't know about you, but I'd like to come out of this thing alive. Yet when I think about all the casualties we took in just the one battle at Cantigny…"

"What do you mean?"

"Andy, we won at Cantigny but we paid quite a price. There's only four of us left from our original ten-man squad at Camp Cotton. Together the 16th and the 28th lost better than two hundred some killed and almost seven hundred wounded.

"Jesus!"

"Yeah, Jesus! So what are our chances when the Heinies start throwing forty or fifty divisions at us? Veteran divisions! That's why I'm fretting, besides all the worries of running this platoon."

"Look," he said, "why don't you go talk to Cap'n Bowcher about it?"

# # #

When I poured out my worries to the captain he said. "Welcome to my world, sergeant."

Then he added, "But try not to lose too much sleep about it, because things may not be quite as bad as they look."

He offered me a cigarette, gave me a light and then lit up his own. "First of all, I want you to know – and be sure to tell the boys this – that General Harbord is being flooded with praise for our fight at Cantigny.

"I mean whether it's from Haig or Foch or the prime minister or any or their subordinates, they're all very impressed by the way we stopped all those Bosche counterattacks cold.

"What's more, we've intercepted some German messages about how disgusted they are with their troops in that fight and surprised how tough we were. We've affected morale on both sides, it seems."

"Sure came at a price, didn't it, Cap'n?"

"It surely did," he said. "But I think you'll be glad to know we're going to get some replacements soon."

"Yessir, and they'll be green as grass," I said.

He gave a wry smile.

"True! But now we can run these novices through some real training programs and not depend upon a bunch of crazy Frogs that no are spik la Engleesh real good."

"Schools, sir?"

He told me the AEF had set up kind of training university near a place called Langres on the Marne River.

"It's a set of practical courses and maybe you and I should do some of them, too. Like the one on camouflage, maybe.

"The replacements will train on that and on how to feed, clean and clear our machineguns and German ones, both for ground operations and against airplanes. They'll work in sapping and mining, about how to use grenades – ours and theirs – and they'll train on flash and sound ranging.

"And Langres also has some training for company-grade officers, among which I want to include you, sergeant. I hear it's quite the place."

He paused.

"There's more," he said, "and it's supposed to be for officers only. But you're in charge of a platoon, so for now at least you're in an officer's position."

"Sir," I said, "maybe we should hold off until the new lieutenant gets here."

"Maybe," he said. "But that might be a while and he'll have a lot to learn. So you might be the only with time to read him in on all this."

"Okay, Cap'n, what are we talking about here?"

He explained that when the 28th drove the Germans out of Cantigny, it came across some German documents. AEF G-2 had them translated and sent out their findings in a memo to infantry and artillery commands.

Captain Bowcher said the German documents spoke of 'Hutier Tactics.'

"From what we hear, these tactics are named after a German general who used the idea against the Russians. It entails fourteen-man squads – they're called *Strumtruppen*…"

"Meaning 'storm troops' I suppose."

"Right, Max. But actually that's a bit of a misnomer. Rather than storming our trenches, as the name suggests, the storm troopers stay low and infiltrate between strong points."

"I get it," I said. "Then they attack from behind or raise all kinds of hell in rear areas, making way for the main assault. I don't see how that really differs from what we've faced all along."

"Well, it differs in that they're given special equipment like light mortars and, especially worrisome, a new light automatic weapon. They call it a machine pistol. Fires a .38 caliber bullet – they call it the 9 mm, same as they use in the Luger. But it fires automatically from a 20-round magazine … say four hundred rounds a minute, or so."

"Damn!"

"Yeah, Max. It can hose down defenders in a trench or fill a bunker with bullets in about two seconds."

"Damn!" I said again. "So what can we do?"

"Backing up first, Max, the thing to remember is that at the sharp end of the spear, all battles -- no matter the size of the forces -- really are small unit actions.

"So your British field manual on hasty fire cover and concealment is very much to the point. And especially so..." -- he slammed his hand on his desk -- "...*especially* so, when you're dealing with infiltration.

"But here's the point. It doesn't matter if they get to the rear if you're already prepped and waiting for them in the rear."

"In *our* rear?"

"Yep, we've come up with some tactics of our own that we think will stymie Herr General Hutier and the whole Imperial German Army."

"I'm all ears, sir."

Chapter 30

Tours – July 1918

"Okay, men, smoke 'em if you' got 'em! And if you don't have 'em ..." I extended my sack of Bull Durham to Sergeant DeVries, "... roll yourself one of mine."

DeVries pulled out a cigarette paper from the package and shook out some of my baccy. Once he licked and rolled his gasper, he looked at me. "Sarge? Got a match?"

"Willie, for God's sake, you're tighter than the bark on a damned tree. What are you going to do with all your money when the Fritzes kill you?"

He grinned as he exhaled, adding to the fog in our bunker. "Taking it with me."

A genial chuckle rumbled from my little NCO group -- Sergeants Hart, Ulrich and Adamczak, plus Corporals Petty, Flannery, VanVoorhees, Sheppard and Titus.

"Okay, boys," I said, "first item on tonight's agenda, we still don't have a lieutenant. Not even a West Point shavetail, so you're stuck with me."

"Oh God, we're screwed," Hart said.

Rubbing his eyes, Ulrich added, "May the good Lord help us." He grinned but looked whipped. They all did because we'd been training our new people day in and day out.

"Okay, guys, any special problems?"

Hart spoke up first. "I'd say the main problem is that the boys seem to think someday soon we'll go over the top and stomp the Bosche. Then it's just On To Berlin."

"Right," Flannery said. "We've got them so they can get their gas masks on in about two seconds, but they don't grasp how important it is.

"They just seem to think its some game or other."

"Plus I've got one wise guy, name of Bright, who keeps telling everybody around him that he's aching for some real action."

That statement produced scornful laughter and a series of acid come-backs. "Ho. Ho. Bright he ain't!" "Now, by 'action', does he mean battle or spending an evening at Madame Celest's House of Ecstasy?"

Adamczak interrupted the laughter.

"I'd keep a close eye on that Bright fellow. Way I see it, the soldier who says he craves action is either lying or a fool. And when guys like that discover what the action really is, they often take to their heels."

"Gents," I said, "the only way I know to get them ready for combat is what you've been doing -- drill, drill, drill and train, train, train until they hate your guts.

"So when the time comes, they react automatically. That's the best way and the only way. It makes them hard-bitten, bitter and tough – which is what foot soldiers need to be."

As they digested that thought, I rolled a cigarette of my own.

"Now the other thing," I said, after lighting up. "We're going to face battle. And right soon.

"Our division, the Big Red One, now is a part of General Gouraud's Fourth Army. Everything we've seen and the fliers I've seen to date show that Ludendorff is getting ready to launch a big new offensive against us. For sure they've got us outnumbered.

"But I'm here to tell you Gouraud has some interesting plans for the Heinies."

"I bet," Petty snorted.

"Now pay attention," I snapped. "This is one very sharp answer to the tactics that have been tearing the British apart on the Somme."

The plan was for a triple-layer defense.

"Each regiment leaves one platoon scattered in the front-line trenches. Gouraud calls it the Sacrifice Line."

"I don't like the sound of that," Adamczak said. "Five gets you ten that we're the ones who will be killed in the general's Sacrifice Line."

"Bill, just listen and quit your bellyaching until you hear the whole plan. To begin with, platoons will rotate in and out of the Sacrifice Line, so it could be anybody who draws the short straw, not just your boys.

"Second, the duty of the men in the Sacrifice Line is not to resist and die to the last man but to shoot Huns and fire flares when the Hun infantry appears ... and then to scoot back to the Intermediate Line.

"When the Germans get into the Sacrifice Line, the French artillery will pound the hell out of it.

"I suspect that will slow the attack because meanwhile, we'll join the rest of the troops in the Intermediate Line. With our rifles and Hotchkisses we'll be picking off the Fritzes as they emerge from the smoke.

"If they get into the Intermediate Line, then we retreat again to the MLR – the Main Line of Resistance. That puts us right back there with the artillery shooting right over our shoulders with open sights."

Ulrich held up a hand. "What if they use gas in our rear area like they've done to the British?"

"They probably will use gas," I said. "That's what our gas masks are for." I got some skeptical looks.

"Yeah, yeah, I know, men! *I know!* It's damned hard to see to aim through those little eye pieces ... especially when they fog up 'cause you're breathing hard. But it beats inhaling mustard gas or choking to death on chlorine.

"Besides, the Bosche will have the same handicap. And you really don't need to aim too well when you throw grenades, do you?"

As they mulled over that remark, I brought up one other little issue.

"Now one last thing men."

"Oh, shit," VanVoorhees said, "here it comes!"

"Right," I said. "Headquarters needs intelligence so tonight we and the frogs are going trench raiding so as to haul in a few squareheads for interrogation."

"We should take Martinez," Ulrich said. "That kid is an artist with a knife, either throwing or slicing."

"What do you mean?"

"Well, play a round of mumblety-peg with him. He can throw a knife so it sticks in exactly the right place. His aim's perfect. He just don't miss. Ever! You lose."

Chapter 31

Tours – July 1918

Instead of mud, the earth on which the men slithered this night was dusty.

When pulling yourself along by your elbows in mud, you get lots of squishing and sucking noises. By comparison, crawling in light, feathery dust is fairly quiet.

…unless you happen to get a snootful that makes you sneeze, something nobody dares do if they want to return in one piece.

I felt a bit guilty about sending the boys on the raid.

By rights, as the platoon's senior NCO I ought to lead them. But temporarily I also was the platoon's commander. So this was one of those times when they say you've got to make hard decisions. You delegate.

"Okay, you'll proceed in two elements," I said. "One to the right. Sergeant Hart, you'll lead. Take DeVries and Guardino and three of the new men -- Campbell, Martin and Vaughan.

"Adamczak is to head the left-hand element. The old hands will be Ulrich and … well, shit, we don't have any other old hands. So take Fothergill, Bright, Sheppard and …

"Sarge," Adamczak interrupted, "I've got dibbies on Vince Martinez, the knife artist."

"Okay. You've got him. So forget Fothergill. Meanwhile, you make sure all your boys have the right weapons – cudgels, grenades, pistols, shore shovels, and the like."

We hiked back to battalion where I made them rehearse their roles again and again. Later the next afternoon, we returned to our front line trench.

"Look, just to review, once the raid strikes…"

The troops and NCOs gave me a lot of eye-rolling.

"I know, dammit, we've been over it and over it. But how else can I tell if you boneheads have it right?

"Now look, the new guys lie at the lip of the trench ready to fire right or left on any relief force. Meanwhile, you old hands drop into the trench and toss grenades into the bunkers.

"After the grenades go off, you dive in, grab documents and any stunned occupants. At the very least, battalion wants unit badges off of the Bosche uniforms.

"Then you head home in relays, *always* with two men hanging back as a rear guard. Got it?"

"Yeah, Sarge, for Christ's sake we got it!"

That was my plan and I really wanted it to work.

But it didn't, of course.

In war, plans never work.

# # #

At 1130 hours, the teams climbed up out of our trench and squirmed into no-man's land.

Their departure left me nervous, smoking and pacing on the duckboards. My little reaction force was hunkered down along the trench trying to sleep.

I suppose I was checking my watch for the twentieth time when a rapid series of grenade blasts horrified me. The explosions came at least ten minutes ahead of the teams' scheduled arrival at the Fritz trench.

"Jesus Christ, did they get ambushed? You men, stand to!"

A few minutes later, just as I decided to take my reaction squad over the top, somebody whistled. He yelled the password and added, "Hey, hold fire! Comin' in! Got some nice juicy Bosches."

Within a half hour, the last of the two teams was back. They bundled their prisoners into my bunker. Nobody in our team got killed. Just two light wounds.

"Our raid started well," Hart told me. "And then it just got better."

He said that the *whump-crump* of the nightly artillery hate drowned the snick of their wire cutters. As Hart clipped a wide tunnel through the barbed wire, Vaughan carefully bent the snipped ends well upward so they couldn't snag weapons or clothes.

"We hadn't gone thirty feet beyond the wire," Hart said, "when Vaughan spotted some squareheads and gave me a little kick. We'd been low-crawling straight toward a squad of Heinies.

"We stopped and listened. Our stall told the other four behind us that something was up. They worked their way beside us so that now we all were in line.

"I whispered, 'Don't move.'

"Sarge, it sounded to me like the Huns were a wire-repair party. I figured it for a god-send, you know. We could attack, snatch a couple of them and be gone, never having to crawl as far as their trenches.

"I wanted to start throwing grenades but when you do that those fuse hammers make a pretty loud 'Crack'. They warn the enemy that in five seconds, something's goin' 'boom!' They might throw their own grenades so instead of a kidnapping we'd have a battle on our hands.

"I hesitated about what to do. But just then we heard a scream off to our left. I reckoned it could be Martinez and his knife. One of the wiring party calls out '*Was ist los*?'

"So smart-ass DeVries here yells out, '*Wer da?*' like he's a German sentry or something. Sarge, that's German for 'Who's there?'"

"No shit, Andy! Will you just get on with it and tell what happened?"

"Sorry, Max. Anyway, counting on DeVries's yell and the scream to confuse the Germans, I shouted "Grenades!" pulled the pin and lofted mine toward the Germans. So did the other guys.

"We pressed ourselves flat. Something clanked – maybe a grenade bounced off a Hun's helmet. Some Fritz said '*Mein Gott!*' and the grenades went off Bam! Bam! Bam! just like a string of big firecrackers.

"Somebody started screaming again from the Germans' direction.

"I meant to yell to grab prisoners but I guess these three bozos panicked. They ran right to us. So we tackled and subdued them and I just yelled to get the hell back to our lines."

Hart said getting his prisoner through the hole in the wire was a bitch. Something kept snagging.

"I pulled hard and heard cloth tear," he said. "I yanked again and, this time, pulled him through with a rush. Vaughan said, 'I got him loose. He was all tangled up with some weapon or other.'

"Anyhow, we waited for the rest of the party to get through the wire and that's pretty much it. I figure the grenades hurt some of the wire party and spooked the three that came running to us."

"Great, Andy!" I said. "How about writing the action report for me?"

"Max, are you kidding? I do the heavy work and you sit back here in this cushy bunker eating bon-bons. Nope, my chores for the night are over."

Chapter 32

Captives – July 1918

Looking around the crowd in the smoky bunker, I said, "Well, congratulations boys. You brought back quite a haul, didn't you? Battalion should be happy."

One prisoner was practically a child, another looked old enough to be my father. The third, a scarred-up corporal, was acting very Prussian, unspeaking, scornful, professional.

Adanczak gestured at the prisoners, "*Sitzen Sie.*" The elder and the younger took a deep collective breath as they seated themselves.

When we offered them cigarettes and coffee, even the Prussian seemed to relax. Sipping greedily, the corporal unbent. "*Kaffee! Ja ganz unglaublich!*" He rattled off something else.

Adamczak translated. "He says it's unbelievable. Said they haven't hadreal coffee since last year."

Adamczak gently asked the youngster, "*Wie alt bist du?*"

The boy murmured something and Adamczak told me, "Jesus, I can't believe it. Born in '03. Poor little runt is only fifteen."

The German corporal jerked his head at the youngster and snorted. "*Ja doch, Sie sind nur Kinder.*"

"What was that?"

"Sarge, he said they're just children. Sounds to me like the Kaiser's scraping the bottom of the barrel."

DeVries piped up. "Yeah, you may be on target. Look at pops here. He's only a private and I'd guess he's at least a good forty years old."

Adamczak found out "pops" was an unhappy forty-four year old draftee. He did his compulsory service from 1892 to 1895 and hadn't expected ever to be in uniform again.

"Here's a knee-slapper. Adamczak said. "Pops wants us to take him to the US of A fast. He claims the German army's about to launch a huge attack upon us. Doesn't want to get trampled when we stampede."

Pops looked depressed when Adamczak explained we turn over the prisoners to the French.

The corporal, a lifer, was a Western Front veteran from back in '14. He seemed relieved to be out of the war. When we asked him to verify an attack was coming, he said he'd only answer questions from officers.

We sent all three to battalion, because another issue was on our minds.

# # #

"Now here's the cherry atop the whipped cream on the sundae," Hart said.

He held up his prize from the raid.

It was a stubby firearm, half the length of any self-respecting rifle. And it had a strange-looking attachment. "Look at this damned thing."

"I think I've heard about this weapon," I said. "It's called a machine pistol, kind of a miniature machinegun. It fires Luger pistol bullets. Look at all the holes in that fitting around the barrel. Ugly damn thing."

"I bet that protects your hands from the hot barrel," Ulrich said. "But what's this other thing?"

"Gotta be the magazine," I said.

"That little drum on the end makes it look like a snail."

"It's ugly, for sure," Adamczak said. "Not near as ugly as a Chauchat, though. Let's try it out."

We took the gun out into the trench. Since Hart captured the weapon, he got to try it first. He yanked back on what looked like a stubby bolt handle. It made a cocking sound.

When he hit the trigger, the gun surprised Hart and the rest of us all by firing a ratta-tat-tat burst.

Then it jammed.

"Smokin' hot momma!" Adamczak said as Hart pulled out the magazine. "So it jams like a Chauchat, but it's a hell of a lot handier. I'd like to have one of these!"

"Right," I said. "If what Pops says is true, you may have the chance pretty soon."

By the time it was my turn, the little machine gun was out of ammo.

Chapter 33

Sacrifice Line – July 1918

The next day our new CO joined us. He was a wiry second lieutenant named Archibald Rupert, fresh from training at Camp Gordon.

I had the platoon brace in ranks to greet him. When he and I exchanged salutes, he said, "Very nice turn-out, sergeant. Thank you. Dismiss the men."

As the troops left for the barn, he smiled and stuck out his hand. "Sergeant Coleman, a pleasure. I mean it. I'm the CO but I'm not sure this is the best time to be taking command."

"Sir?"

He took a breath. "Regiment says we're on alert as of now."

"On alert, Sir?"

"Yep. Aeroplane spotters report large columns of troops building up in the German First Army, ten or so divisions. Large piles of boats. Prisoners say their mission is to cross the Marne to drive straight for Paris. They'll attack this sector right after midnight two days from now."

I tilted my helmet back. "Hoo, boy, that chimes with what we hear! Sir, couldn't you bring us some good news?"

He chuckled. "When I hear any good news, Max, you'll be first on my list.

"But here's the thing: there's not much time for me to get to know the platoon. So even though I'm the new CO, you're the experience, the veteran. So we'll carry on just as you have been. No changes for the moment. Meanwhile, fill me in in the platoon. After that, if we have time, I want to meet the NCOs."

"Okay, sir," I said. "Well, very quickly, this platoon has a solid cadre of veteran NCOs. Some of us have been with the outfit since before Mexico. We also have a large number of very eager fairly tough but green soldiers. They're in good condition and they think they're eager for battle.

"Just one problem," I added.

"What's that?"

Looking him right in the eyes, I said, "None has ever been in real combat."

He looked straight back. "Me neither, sergeant."

"So," I said, "looks like we're going to find out a lot about our platoon."

"And ourselves," he added.

"Sir," I said, "all this news is scary, but I think we'll do okay. I've only known one of these kids who didn't measure up when the time came."

# # #

Two nights later I was crouched in the trench. For the tenth time I ran through my mental check list to get the platoon ready: ammo, water, bandages, rations, first aid, stretchers…

The lieutenant startled me by looming out of the darkness. "Sergeant, do you normally smoke two butts at once? I can't believe it's good for your wind."

I glanced up at his silhouette against the night sky. Then I became conscious of the cigarette in my right hand and looked at the other glowing in a butt niche in the trench wall.

I gave a guffaw. "You caught me, sir. I guess, being's how we're in General Gouraud's Sacrifice Line, I figured the more fags I smoked the faster the time would go and the sooner we'd get this over with."

We and our troops were waiting out the clock for midnight and the German onslaught.

"Makes sense," the lieutenant said. "Maybe that's why I tried to take up smoking today. Got to have something to do while you wait … "

"Yes sir…wait to be sacrificed."

"You've got your flare gun? Mine's ready to fire."

"Yessir, locked and loaded. Guardino and Adamczak each have one, too."

Just I was about to ask whether he wanted some Bull Durham, our world seemed to detonate. To the west dozens of bright orange flashes heralded a tremendous ground-shaking *Whamp! Whamp! Whamp!*

The pounding roar came from dozens of General Gouraud's howitzer batteries. They'd sprung a surprise barrage upon the Germans who were staging to attack. The drumbeat of muzzle blasts half deafened us. Their vibration caused little crumbles of dirt to trickle from our trench wall.

The shells tore overhead and seconds later came more flashes and then *thud, thud, thud* – a drumfire of French artillery rounds bursting in the German lines on the far side of the Marne.

"Hot damn!" Lieutenant Rupert shouted through the uproar. "We're shelling them first! That's got to be a very nasty surprise for the Fritzes."

I yelled back, "Great, Sir! Now how about a cigarette?"

"Thanks."

# # #

With the hands on my watch ticking toward 2400, I spoke through the roar to the lieutenant, "Sir, supposedly the Bosche will begin their barrage any minute."

"Right," he answered, sounding as tense as I felt.

"Sir, a word to the wise. When shelling starts you want to keep your mouth open. Protects the ear drums, somehow."

He nodded. "Gotcha, Sarge."

"Another thing, sir. Even though a barrage is really noisy, your ears learn pretty quickly. They get so they can tell you what's coming and give you a good idea of where it'll land."

"For real, Max?"

"Yessir, takes some practice. Just follow us for now!"

He held up a thumb and nodded again.

Right after midnight, the first shells in the German barrage began blasting around us. The shock waves were as jarring as being body blocked.

One shell exploded just shy of our trench. A shower of reeking dirt fell down onto us. You could taste the cordite in the dust.

I leaned close to the lieutenant and yelled, "Right now they're throwing those big shells at us. Hear that tearing sound as they come down? Probably a 150 mm howitzer. We call 'em Jack Johnsons."

"Why?"

"Because they hit big and hard like that champion Negro boxer."

He nodded jerkily. Then we both ducked as another "Johnson" slammed maybe ten feet from the lip of our trench, collapsing part of it onto us.

We struggled upward through the soil's weight to get back to our feet. We shook our heads and slapped the dirt from our bodies.

I said, "Sir, I'll shut up after this, but keep alert for quiet shells -- mortars – plus those damned 77s. Mortars don't make much noise coming in, but they're the real daisy-cutters. Slice you to bits. I think they kill the most people."

"Please *don't* shut up," he yelled back. "Keep your class going."

Chapter 34
Skedaddling – July 1918

Just then a deep-voiced metallic clangor began -- somebody hammering a big brass artillery shell casing.

Clawing my mask carrier open, I yelled, "Gas alarm, sir! Masks on!"

I bellowed "Gasssss! Gaaassssss!" first to the right, then to the left along the trench.

Others took up the same call, but only briefly. The big shells' approaching howl speeded us in doffing our helmets. The gas shells landed with muted explosions -- an anti-climatic *pyunnng* -- as they spewed out their contents. We yanked the respirators over our heads.

Darkness became inky as the mask enfolded my face.

I gripped the breathing tube between my teeth, then clipped the pinchers onto my nose and pulled the fabric and straps over my head.

Gambling that gas hadn't reached us, I unscrewed the lid from a tiny tin and stuck a fingertip into it. Reaching into the mask, I spread a thin coat of glycerin inside the lenses to keep them from fogging.

As I refitted the mask I caught a faint whiff of chlorine. *Thank God it's not mustard gas!*

It had been a lark to play ball while wearing a gas mask. But during a gas attack, -- especially at night -- it's a wide-awake nightmare.

Masks isolate. You can't speak or yell. Vision's poor at best. Even in an earth-quaking barrage, you hear little but your own fevered panting … and maybe your prayer, "*Dear God, please make sure that the charcoal filter works.*"

We mounted the firing step, rifles cocked, heads and eyes whipping right, then left, and right again trying to strain through the pall of dust and smoke, trying to penetrate the fog of gas itself.

Faint shapes appeared and vanished, flickering silhouettes against the brief flashes of artillery bursts on the German line.

Strumtruppen!

Riflemen, men with machine pistols, others straining to carry small mortar tubes or Maxim machine guns. We saw shapes of men with paddles – small boats landing on our side of the river.

We all began firing.

It was too dark to use our rifle sights, but we brought down some of the ghostly figures. As more appeared, our Hotchkiss machinegun team hammered at the silhouettes – one man at the grips and trigger, the other feeding in the ammo strips.

Through the smoke more groups appeared, pistol-carrying officers waving their men on.

A sudden orange light flared off to our left. Flamethrower! The flame was indistinct in the smoke but the screams weren't. The orange light tapered off and bloomed again, showering east to west.

Trying to aim just off the flare, we hoped to hit the man or the tanks he was carrying. The Hotchkiss gunner blasted two strips, forty rounds, at the orange glare. He earned a large explosion and then the faint sight of a man afire trying to run from his own blaze.

If the destruction of the *Flammenwerfer* discouraged our attackers you'd never know it. We glimpsed more silhouettes running hard, coming closer.

"It's time," I told myself. I pointed my flare gun vertically and fired. It signaled the Intermediate Line that the Bosche assault was reaching the Sacrifice Line.

The flare also signaled our platoon to start racing back to the Intermediate Line.

A helmeted head with its monkey face turned toward me … the lieutenant in his gas mask. I reloaded the gun with a new flare and fired. Then as he fired his flare, I waved to the rear. He did the same. We began climbing the rear of the trench.

A crimson flash erupted to our right in our trench. The blast catapulted a little American with rifle and a football – Fothergill with his Enfield and the cat imprisoned in its gas mask.

The lieutenant and I were beyond that shell's lethal range, but its shrapnel stung us both on our right sides and arms.

# # #

When masked and in darkness, you're three-fourths blind forcing us to cross shelled ground at a trot rather than a sprint.

At least the lieutenant and I had company – a thick-bodied Yank, Guardino maybe, plus shadowy shapes that moved like DeVries, Campbell, Reese and Petty

Campbell slapped my arm and pointed to the left.

Maybe ten yards away, two Fritzes were in the act of fitting a Maxim machinegun to a tripod mount being steadied by a third man. As I yanked a pin from a grenade, I dimly made out several other troops bent over, perhaps opening ammo cartons.

When the grenade exploded, we charged into the smoke with bayonets. We'd never drilled this, but the same fury drove us: *Kill the bastards before they get that goddam gun working.*

The grenade wounded or killed the men with the gun and shocked several others.

My own target tried to stand and fumbled with his Mauser. I felt bone cave when I butt-smashed his head just below the helmet rim. A Fritz collapsed with wracking coughs when Gardino ripped away his gas mask.

Two loud cracks and Lieutenant Rupert's .45 leveled another gunner. We were so battle-mad we hardly heard a fusillade -- DeVries and his Chauchat trading bursts with two Heinies and their little machine guns.

DeVries and the Chauchat won.

Considering all that they had to carry, Bosche machine gun crews usually operated with nine men. We weren't counting. Reese drove his bayonet through the gun's water jacket and we took off again, running for the Intermediate Line

It seemed like hours before we arrived. Our troops in those trenches wore no masks so with tremendous relief we ripped ours off, taking in huge gasps of clean, fresh air. Perhaps the Bosche didn't gas the Intermediate Line because they didn't know about it.

I was glad to see Adamczak and Ulrich arrive in our wake. In the next twenty minutes Martinez, and DeVries came tumbling into our trench.

"Anybody seen Sheppard?"

Petty said, "Sarge, he stopped one just as we climbed out of the trench. And I think the Bosche captured Titus and Bright."

"Well, that's life in the PFI," Guardino said.

"The what?"

"Poor Fucking Infantry. By the way, Sarge, you and the lieutenant are doing a bit of bleeding."

"Just flesh wounds," I said. "We'll get it checked once the battle is over."

As of mid-morning, it became evident that the German assault pretty much stalled in the Sacrifice Line.

Columns of Fritzes kept appearing out of the line's banked-up smoke. We flensed them with rifle and machinegun fire and air and ground-bursts from French artillery. By day's end, the Huns gave up.

General Gouraud's defense in depth stopped them cold.

Chapter 35

Behind The Marne – July 1918

Lieutenant Rupert and I and four other walking wounded headed back to an aid station.

The aid station was a long stone milking shed packed with wounded – some crying aloud, some still and quiet, other sitting, smoking and lying to each other about how they got their injuries.

A nurse glanced at our right arms and sides. "No blood on y'all's trousers," she said. "Best peel off them rags right now so's I can take a look-see." The right sleeves and sides of both our shirts looked riddled, as if mice had been at them.

I asked the nurse, "By any chance are y'all from Takes-iss?"

"Yep,' she said, never taking her eyes from the lieutenant's right arm and side. "But don't be getting any funny notions," she added, giving my carcass a quick look.

"I'll apply iodine so your punctures don't get infected and we'll give you a tetanus shot. If I have time, I'll take out the shrapnel."

"Then surgeons won't see us?" Lieutenant Rupert asked.

Turning to Reese, she snorted. "They been workin' since midnight on serious wounds – terrible wounds, faces burst, intestines torn out, legs ripped off. Don't worry. Us nurses do some of the surgery, too, and we sure know how to sew gashes shut. We can take good care of y'all."

She helped Reese out of his field shirt which was sopping with blood.

"Whoa, fella," she said, "you stopped a good-sized one. You boys help lay him down on his left side. Be easy. No jerking."

As the lieutenant raised the legs from the floor I helped lower Reese's torso to the table. Reese caught his breath. "Like she said, guys, go easy."

"Awww pipe down, Reese, You ain't in any position to go giving orders to your first shirt and commander."

"Bullshit," he said in a quivery voice. "I been hit so I'm outside the chain of command now."

"Like hell you are, Reese. You're still in the Army."

The lieutenant said, "Both of you stop yammering. That's a direct order."

Once we had Reese on his side, blood streamed down across his back from a long red slit near the base of his rib cage.

"Good. Good," she said. "Y'all stay with him jest a second. Be right back."

She stepped to a supply stand and came back quickly, fingers inside the dual rings of a large hypodermic needle. "Jes' a little shot here," she said, inserting the needle beside the wound. "An' another'n there, an' then another'n rightcheer."

Reese clamped his lips and held his breath for each injection.

I said, "Now you'll feel better, Reese."

Eyes still wide, he nodded. The nurse placed a thick strip of gauze over his wound. "Okay, he'll do for a minute. Now some iodine for you boys. By then he'll be all numbed up."

Using more gauze, she smeared iodine liberally up and down our arms and sides. It was cool but stung viciously. We followed Reese's clenched-teeth example, neither of us giving a murmur.

"Now, your turn to help," she said, pointing to the lieutenant. "Come over here and get a grip on his feet. Hold real tight and keep them immobile.

"And you, sergeant. Pull his arm up over y'all's own shoulder and behind your neck. Hold that arm with your left hand and brace your other forearm accrost his armpit. When I say 'Pull!' y'all slowly stretch his shoulder toward you and don't be lettin' him jerk.

"Mr. Reese," she said, "y'all do your best to hold perfectly still now. But I have to say this could hurt a mite."

"This" meant shoving the nickle-plated jaws of a forceps into the rent in Reese's side. She commanded, "Pull!" I pulled, hauling his shoulder toward me, widening the wound.

Reese went as rigid as a length of railway track. Between his teeth, he groaned, *Aaaaaaaaaggh! Damn! Damnnnnn!*

Suddenly she said. "It's over. Lookie here!"

The forceps held a slightly-curved steel wedge about an eighth-inch thick and two inches wide. Parts of Reese clung to some of its frilled edges.

"Lucky it didn't go right through y'all," she said. "Now you boys keep aholt of him because I got to see if they's any cloth or other debris still down in there. Won't take but a couple of seconds."

It seemed to me to take five minutes. I suspect it felt like an hour to Reese.

"We're done," she announced at last.

Reese asked anxiously, "Don't you sew it shut?"

"Not yet," she said. "I'll sprinkle Acriflaven in it. Helps stop infections. Then we might put you on a Dakin drip. But you should heal up real nice.

"Now, you two," she said to the lieutenant and me. "I've got to get them little chunks of iron and pebbles out'n your hides."

"Hey, Sister," Reese cracked, "you need me to hold them for you?"

"We'll see," she chuckled. "Now, who's first?"

"Lieutenant Rupert," I said, bowing toward him. "Rank has precedence."

"Very thoughtful of you sergeant," he replied, "but incorrect. Article 48, Subsection B, paragraph 5 of Field Service Regulations mandates that officers give way to enlisted men in hospitals."

Days later I went to the book and found no references to hospitals in Article 48.

The nurse, who identified herself as Sister Ellen, took a pair of tweezers and, frequently dipping them in alcohol, worked her way down my ribs and then up my right arm. I looked away as she plucked out small bits of steel and occasional pieces of grit.

Debriding me and the lieutenant, she filled a coffee mug with tiny bits of shrapnel and what she called miscellaneous grit. Then it was time for another iodine wash.

By now the cuffs of her white gown were reddish brown with blood. She also had a red streak on her right forehead after trying with her wrist to push a stray lock of hair from her eyes.

No, she wasn't from El Paso but some other border town named Brownsville, I believe. No, she didn't have a fella.

"And I'm not about to have one," she said, "until this horrid war is over. Then I'll marry me a rich doctor."

"Maybe you ought to become a doctor," I said. "You really seem to know what you're doing."

"A woman doctor?" She snorted again. "Now listen, you two," she said. "With all those little wounds, you're likely to get infected. So no shirts for today and keep your arms out from your sides. We're out of beds, so have a seat out on the grass. Stay out in the clean air. And rest, sleep if you can. Come back at dusk for more iodine."

Before we could answer, she turned back to set up Reese's Dakin Drip, whatever that was.

# # #

After we left the aid station, Lieutenant Rupert said, "Max, you ought to stay in touch with Sister Ellen. I think she likes you."

"Paaaah," I responded. "Sir, she wouldn't be interested in some nobody sergeant. She wants to marry a rich doctor."

"I don't know about that, Max. I think your idea that she become a doctor rocked her a bit. Showed her you're interested in something more than a roll in the hay."

"Maybe," I said, "but I'm only an Indiana farm boy from the stock yards. I've got naught to offer her but a sergeant's pay."

Chapter 36

Recuperating — July 1918

Though Sister Ellen ordered us to rest, doing so near the aid station wasn't easy. It's hard to nap or even relax when screams and moans of the wounded keep coming to you.

Equally distracting were the piercing cracks coming to us from a four-gun battery two hundred yards away. It was hammering incessantly at the Germans.

After trying to loll about in the sunshine for an hour, the lieutenant said, "Come on. Let's go take a look at that battery."

So we each chewed two pieces of gauze to serve as ear plugs and wandered toward the four guns which were firing over a large berm.

A stocky little major wearing rimless glasses approached us. Just as we saluted he asked, "Who the hell are you men?"

"Sorry, sir, we're with the 16th Infantry. I'm Lieutenant Rupert and this is First Sergeant Coleman. We're out of uniform because of doctor's orders -- some minor wounds.

"I wanted to show Sergeant Coleman what artillery in action is like. This is the sergeant's first opportunity for a close-up look at saucy cans."

The major chuckled. "You men are welcome to watch. Just stay out of the way. We're very busy trying to make life miserable in the Bosche rear." He walked away.

Each time one of the guns fired, that hard *Crack!* jarred me. It made me flinch and duck my head.

The battery looked busy as a bee hive – except that it was a thousand times as noisy with the unremitting blasts from the four cannon.

Ammunition handlers raced back and forth to carry shells from the ammo wagons to the gun breeches.

"Those ammo runners look to me like they really earn their pay," I said.

"You bet they do," the lieutenant said. "I know from painful experience because we did a quite a bit of time with those cannon at Camp Gordon."

"So, sir, did I hear you call the guns saucy cans?"

"Right, Max. These are direct fire field guns – 75 mm. In French the number 75 is pronounced something like *swasahn-khan*. But the boys just call them 'saucy cans' because they don't read or speak French, and won't even try to pronounce it right

"But at Camp Gordon we never fired the guns this fast. I'd say each of these crews is getting off twenty rounds a minute or a touch more."

Two men sat on steel seats either side of each gun's breech. The man on the left adjusted the gun's elevation and traverse wheels. The man on the right did nothing but pull and release the firing lanyard.

"Looks to me like the guys on the right with the lanyards have the easy job."

The lieutenant told me, "Don't you believe it, Max!

"If you look close you notice they aren't just seated. They lean to brace their right shoulders against the gun shield so, to help brace themselves, they've stiffened their left legs way out and dig their left feet into the ground to support themselves.

"This gun has a great recoil system. But that shoulder against the shield keeps the gun from rocking back even a little bit on its wheels. Keeps the gun on target.

"The trouble is that the gunner can't help but breathe smoke coming from the breech every time the loader opens it and pulls out the old casing.

"It gives you a bitch of headache in about five minutes and that muzzle blast six feet from your ears doesn't help, either."

"I'm sure it's a tough job, Lieutenant. But it looks a good deal safer than going over the top into machinegun fire."

"That's for sure," he said. "But if the Bosche airmen spot the location of this battery and get the word back to Fritz's heavy guns, it's a whole 'nother story."

"I get your point," I said.

It still looked to me like the loaders had the toughest job, pulling the shells from the magazine and running 30 feet with them to the gun.

On arrival, they opened the breech, yanked out the empty casing, tossed it eight or ten feet to the rear, slammed in the new shell and closed the breech all the while getting their own deep breath of eau de cordite.

The lieutenant looked more closely. "One good thing. The gunners at least have ear plugs."

"Ear plugs?"

"Yep. They call 'em ear defenders. Either brass or wood. They help a quite bit so's your ears don't ring so bad. There's been talk of issuing them to rifle companies."

# # #

The next morning, sore as hell from the scabs on our little wounds, we gingerly tried on new uniform shirts.

A truck delivered us to the 16th Infantry back at our barn barracks.

I returned to the company to check the casualty list, meet replacements and start requisitioning or scrounging for lost equipment.

Meanwhile the lieutenant was ordered off to a hush-hush conference of the regiment's officers.

I knew Sheppard and Fothergill probably were dead and Reese, Petty, Converse, Bright and Motley all were wounded. Converse wouldn't be back and I considered Reese a question mark. A wound that deep might go morbid.

Missing, presumed captured, were Titus and VanVoorhees.

I was glum in looking over the butcher's bill when somebody hesitantly said, "Uh, first sergeant? They told us we should report to you."

Speaking was a smiling, gangly six-footer with a lantern jaw. His uniform and all his gear looked brand new.

"So," I said, "report."

The smile again, "Sir, I'm Private David Crockett and these here boys are Eddie Harrison, Fred Andrews, Harry VanderStelt, Woody Johnson and this here little guy is Vince Zimmer."

"First off, Crockett, don't call me 'sir'. I'm not an officer. I work for a living. So, Davy Crockett, eh? Are you a great shot?"

"Sergeant, I'm tolerable out to about four hunnert yards. After that not so hot, but Eddie here shoots real good at six hunnert. Fred here ain't so bad, neither. But little Zimmer is best of all of us."

Zimmer looked to me to be about five-three and might weigh 120 if soaking wet. He had the innocent face of a twelve-year-old.

"Zimmer," I said, "can you even *carry* a rifle?"

He gave me a cold look. "Sarge, I can do a lot more with a rifle than just carry it. But I can do that too -- for up to 20 miles."

"Okay, Zimmer, if you say so. We'll see.

"Meanwhile," I said, "welcome to all of you to A Company. For now you six will take over the duties of nine men who were killed, wounded or captured the night before last."

Crockett's smile faded. Zimmer gulped.

"So," Johnson said with a leer, "we're gonna pay the bastards back. *I'm* ready!" The others exchanged glances.

"Men," I said, "I'm glad to hear you're good shots, but in the trenches we usually have to fight dirty. We rely a lot on grenades. And a spiked club or short-handled shovel or a real sharp bayonet is just about as useful as an Enfield."

I gave them a minute to digest that information.

"What I want you boys to do now is look up Sergeant Hart, Andy Hart, and he'll get you situated. We're off the line for a day or two, but I kind of suspect we'll go back to join the trench rabbits before long."

Crockett asked, "Trench rabbits?"

"Yeah," I said. "Back in civilization, folks call them rats."

Harrison went pale and said, "Ewwww. Are the rats big?"

With a straight face I said, "Oh, I'd say usually about the size of a cat. We heard that up north the Atkinses import ferrets to deal with them."

"The Atkinses?"

"Right, that's Tommy Atkins, the nickname for soldiers in the British Expeditionary Force.

"You'll also hear the word Poilu, for the French soldiers. We call 'em Frogs – but not to their faces. We Americans are Yanks, of course, or doughboys and sometimes even Teddies, though I don't know why."

"Damn," Zimmer said, "we've got a lot to learn."

"Don't worry," I said. "You're going to be in combat, one of the toughest schools of all. You learn fast, if you survive."

"Bring 'em on," Johnson said.

Zimmer gulped again.

Chapter 37

Grim Notice — August 1918

When he called us NCOs together, Captain Bowcher looked pensive. "Men, the easy part of this war is over."

I felt others around me stir. Somebody muttered, "The *easy* part?"

The captain let his statement gnaw at us a few seconds.

"Yes, the easy part. So far, we've done most of our fighting on defense. We just helped blunt a German offensive. Before that at Cantigny, I grant you, we had to advance a ways against Bosche fire. But even then our mission was to defend our comrades who already captured that little burg.

"Well, soon we're going to start attacking, not to defend some pile of rubble, but to attack and keep attacking until we defeat the Bosche for good."

He told us the allies, now under a single command – Marshall Foch – had developed a grand strategy to attack constantly from sector to sector.

"First I'm told we're going to force the Fritzes out of the big salient they created in their spring and summer offensives.

"We helped halt their attack across the Marne. And we're still here at the furthest point they reached…at the tip of the salient, if you like.

"Well very soon, we're going to convoy north with the rest of First Division to attack the west shoulder of that salient. Our objective is to cut the road and railway between Soissons and Chateau-Thierry – it's their only major supply route. When we cut it, they'll have to retreat and abandon that salient. That's attack number one.

"I don't know the details," he said, "and I won't ever see any detailed plans. But the idea is that from now on the French will attack one week, the Tommies the next and us the next and so on. The point is to wear down the Bosche by forcing them to switch forces from threat to threat."

"Beg pardon, sir," I said, "but won't that tend to wear us down, too?"

"You're exactly right, first sergeant. That's why I said the easy part is over.

"We're going to have to move quickly. But the point is that with us Yanks here, the allies for the first time now come close to parity in manpower with the Fritzes."

He told us Ludendorff's spring offensives – including the one we helped stop – had bled the German army. "It's not the same army that it was even last year," He said. "And the allied blockade has begun to starve the German homeland.

"Even so, the Germans still are tough soldiers and it's going to take hard fighting to capture Berlin."

# # #

As we walked away from the briefing, Andy Hart said, "Capture Berlin my ass! This stinking war has been underway in northeast France four fucking years. And do you know how far it is from here to Berlin?"

"No idea," I said. "But keep your grousing to yourself and me. Don't start discouraging the troops."

"Yeah," he said. "We wouldn't want them to know their chances of coming out alive are just about zero."

"Dammit, Andy, stuff that kind of talk! We're for sure going to lose some of them, but that's the business you and I signed up for. And, remember, they volunteered. Look, buddy, they *wanted* this fight! Remember all that blather about killing Kaiser Bill?"

He gave me a furious look.

"Besides, Andy, the high command knows a hell of a lot more about this than you and I do."

"I wonder, Max," he said. "I really wonder. But just for your information, from this point it's more'n five hundred miles to Berlin and nobody – I mean *nobody* – has gained more four or five miles at a time against the Heinies in four solid years."

"Yep. So keep your damned yap shut about it! Is that clear?"

The order earned me another glare.

# # #

Andy's bitterness fed my own doubts, but when I reported to Captain Bowcher, he buried them in business. "Top," he said, "it looks like you've got two days to get the men ready for a hard march. We'll back you up when need be."

I said, "No need, sir. They'll be ready." I immediately dived into the thousand-and-one details in bringing an infantry company back up to snuff.

Ninety-first on my list was a full equipment inspection, First Platoon first. Andy had his boys in a spread formation, each man standing, his field pack opened on the ground in front of him, all equipment laid out on the ground exactly by regulation, making it simple to spot deficiencies.

"You idiot!" I exploded to the third kid in line.

I bellowed at Private Harrison because he'd stuffed his gas mask carrier with candy.

"You simpleton! Where the hell is your gas mask?"

"I left it back in the barn. See sarge, I like to keep a sucker in my mouth when I'm marching and . . ."

"Jesus *Christ*!" I knocked off his helmet and yanked the carrier's straps up over his head. I dumped the candies and ground them into the soil with my heel.

"Give me fifty push-ups right here, young trooper! When you reach fifty, run upstairs in the barn. Get your gas mask. Put it on. Then come down and run around the barn five times. Run *fast*! Then you return to ranks and give me fifty more. Now *drop*!"

"Crockett, you keep count to make sure he follows these orders to the letter!"

"Yes, sergeant!"

As he started his push-ups, I said, "You know, Harrison, you may get a bit short of breath by the time you're back. Well that's nothing compared to inhaling chlorine or mustard gas."

I stepped further back from the front of the formation. "Everybody! Put on your gas masks!"

Four other people couldn't.

Two chow hounds had crammed their mask carriers with French loaves and sausages. Another had candy and the fourth man had stuffed his carrier with cash. Poker winnings, he said.

I confiscated the money, saying he'd receive it when he received his discharge pay after the war.

"And now, you stupid bastards, the same routine. Drop and give me fifty! Then head for the barn!"

For a minute I grinned inside about how much I now sounded like Corporal McKinnis five years back at Jefferson Barracks.

Andy couldn't suppress his own chuckles as the two of us resumed our close examination of the open field packs.

A day later he told me the recruits had nicknamed me. They spoke of me as Sergeant Clawman.

Chapter 38

Getting Set – July '18

"I think God must be on Germany's side after all."

Brushing the water from my face, I said, "Crockett, what the hell makes you say a thing like that?"

"Well, Sarge, no sooner did we pile out of those camion trucks and start to march than the rain started up – that very danged minute. And it ain't stopped."

"And neither have we," Andrews added.

"We aren't going to stop either," I growled.

"Gee, don't rub it in, Sarge."

It was a dreary late afternoon. Rain slanted into our faces as we toiled on foot toward Soissons under full packs and ammunition loads.

The rim of Crockett's helmet streamed with the rattling rain, just like everyone else's. He lurched as he walked and so did the rest of us

The lurching was the refugees' fault.

Our regiment marched east while a thick column of terrified French citizens fled west on the same road. Most seemed to be farm folk. Many looked old, like grandparents. They limped beside farm carts or hay wagons drawn by skinny old sway-backed horses. Small children perched in the wagons amid household treasures, ornate clocks and big-horned gramophones.

All of us, soldiers and civilians, stopped to bow – we were too tired to fall and get back up – when the occasional shrill shriek and crash marked the arrival of a German shell. The artillery fire was sporadic and usually, thank God, landed fifty to a hundred feet from the road.

Refugees took up most of the road, leaving the shoulders to us. The rain was eroding the shoulders meaning one leg had to bend deep with each stride because the opposite foot was in mud six to twelve inches lower.

That was the lurch.

Andrews complained. Everybody complained when they had the breath. But Andrews was clearest in his gripe.

"Now, Sarge, most of us is used to marching. Got good hard feet. We've marched just about ever'where and in all kind of weathers. But toting forty pound of gear and lurching all twenny miles or so is another story. Don't you think we ought to take a break, Sarge?"

It really was a bitch of a hike, and you really couldn't blame the refugees. They all looked soaked and pathetic, especially the children.

"I sure don't want a break," I lied, as another shell crashed in the mud to our left. "I *like* marching this way. In fact, if I had the energy I'd climb up onto one of those farm wagons and just sleep.

"But General Bullard needs us to be in the Compiegne Forest by dawn. We've got to link up with the Moroccans and parts of the Yank Second Division. So 16th Infantry is taking no breaks."

Adamzcak added sourly, "So quit your whining, Andrews. We're all tired."

We did take an brief unintentional break when I came upon Guardino holding a sobbing, shivering little girl, maybe a three-year-old. Rain had plastered black ringlets to her delicate skull.

"Guardino, what the hell are you doing with that child?"

"Sarge, she was just crying here at roadside all by her lonesome. Poor thing's barefoot, too. I tried to hand her off to the refugees. They wouldn't take her. I couldn't just march off and leave her."

"So, you were planning to take her to help us fight the Bosche?"

"Hell, no. I figured to just maybe drop her off at a farm."

"I bet most farms hereabouts are abandoned." I took the girl from him. She came willingly, laid her face against my neck stirring up a storm of memories and emotions. I tucked her little feet into the shirt beneath my gas mask carrier.

Crockett, Zimmer and Harrison stopped to gather round. "Darlin', I'd give you a bon-bon," Harrison said, "but mean ole Sarge wouldn't let me bring none."

"There, there, sweetie," Crockett said. He reached out to touch her hand. "Ole Clawman'll take good care of you."

She looked away from him and buried her face in my neck again. I gently swayed side-to-side with her.

"Crockett," I said, "I know you mean well, but your phizz is *so* damned ugly…"

He laughed. "Right, Sarge. Parents back to home used to hire me to scare their kids with my mug."

"Alright, Boys," I said. "Enough chatter. Keep marching. Little Missy and I are right with you. I've got to find someone for her. Maybe some MPs."

Guardino said, "Whoa, Sarge! Don't you be turning this little sweetie over to them hairy-assed bastards."

"Hey, Guardino, watch your language!"

"Sarge, for Christ's sake, she don't know English! But I was gonna say Engineers might be better. They could fix up some kind of shelter for her."

"Good idea."

I finally met an artillery sergeant who arranged for Missy to ride with an artillery lieutenant headed back west in an empty ammo truck. Being the father of twin girls, the officer was happy to help.

Not long after dark, the last of the refugees was gone and we had the road to ourselves … and the rain.

"How much longer 'till we get to them Campaign woods, Sarge?"

"It's Compiegne, Crockett. And you don't want to know how much longer. Just keep on stepping out."

Martinez behind me was muttering, "Boots! Boots! Boots! Movin' up and down again …"

"Vince, where'd you hear that poem?"

"Don't know it to be a poem, Sarge. I just heard somebody sayin' it and it helps me keep going."

"'Boots' is a whole poem by an Englishman named Rudyard Kipling. You ought to read it."

"If I make it out alive, I will read it. But right now it's all I can do is hike."

"Right you are."

The pace had me worried. We'd been traveling north all day, first by camion, then foot. I reckoned we'd have to march at least six more miles, meaning we'd be utterly exhausted just in time to assault the Bosche.

About 0400 Captain Bowcher and a guide directed us off the road. "Get some rest in the woods while you can. The ground's wet, but you can't get any more soaked than we are now."

As the men turned off the road, the captain anxiously asked me, "How are the boys?"

"Sir, they're whipped. But they're young and pretty tough. I think they'll do okay with a little sleep."

"Damned little," he said. "Our barrage starts in an hour."

As he spoke, a column of small tanks roared and clanked past us spewing muddy rooster tails from their tracks.

I hobbled along the line. It was difficult to tell in the dark, but the platoon sergeants told me we'd lost very few stragglers. After reporting back to the captain, I sat down against the trunk of a big tree and fell asleep.

Chapter 39

Assaulting – July 1918

Something weird about me … maybe hatred of being startled awake. I always awaken minutes before buglers start tootling reville.

On this particular morning, I awakened before several dozen French howitzer batteries roared *Bon jour* to the Bosche. The guns' targets were German troops occupying the heights overlooking roads and rail lines connecting Soissons to Chateau-Thierry.

Our job was to cut that supply route. Multiple flashes from artillery muzzles were bright enough for me to see the troops jerk bolt upright, startled out of their exhausted sleep. Others slept so deeply we had to kick them awake.

Through the groaning and bitching, I yelled, "Great news! The rain quit…mostly." Nobody seemed in a mood to give thanks.

"Right, men! Leave your packs. All we need today is rifles, ammo and grenades. We've got three minutes to eat some bully beef."

Andy spat. "Aktooie! I'll settle for coffee."

"No fires," I said. "We want to surprise the Huns so no coffee."

By dawn B Company was scrambling through the mist and drizzle about a hundred yards behind a squadron of the small tanks. Captain Bowcher was ten yards in the lead.

Above the growl of gunfire and tank motors, screams surprised us. But they weren't screams from wounded men. The shrill ululations were cheers of a sort – or maybe war whoops. They came from our buddies, the Moroccan infantry to our right.

We got to know and like Moroccan poilus late last year. Aside from being tough veterans they were kind of a traveling road show -- black Africans, Canuks, Saharan Arabs, Asians from China and Indo-China, a few foreign legionnaires and even a scattering of Yanks.

They wore turbans or fezzes and some trotted along in very baggy pants reminding me the old Union Army Civil War zouaves.

Waving their direction, Captain Bowcher said, "I'm glad to have them next door. They know their business."

For once, few shell holes lay before us, so we advanced across fairly level ground. Even so the terrain was anything but flat. Deep ravines broke up the hills to our front. And dozens of deep gullies scored the shoulders of those ravines.

Orange flickers began erupting half-way up those slopes along with the high-speed thudding of German machineguns.

Bullets pocked the muddy ground at our feet, but the tanks' gunners zeroed in on the Maxim nests. We were able to clamber up the ravines with light losses.

Two injuries, however, rattled me to the core. Our exec, Lieutenant Rupert, went down when a mortar fragment ripped a huge chunk of meat from his left thigh. He didn't yell or moan, but the sweat and fixed look on his face showed his agony.

Then just as we crested the V-top of a ravine, an 8 mm Maxim bullet to the chest spun Captain Bowcher to the ground.

His aide, a headquarters corporal, started tearing open the captain's shirt. Sputtering blood, the captain snapped, "Quit that!" He snatched at my trouser leg and pointed east with the other hand. "See that, Top?"

"Look! Bosche artillery! We're in their rear. Total surprise! You command. Keep them going. Cut that rail line."

"Yessir! We'll keep going."

He ordered the corporal, "Give Top my map!" Turning frantic eyes on me, "It's victory, sergeant! Keep going! All costs!"

I waved forward to everybody I saw. I told the kneeling corporal. "Stay here. Bandage him and get help for him. That's an order!"

# # #

By 1000 I guessed we'd penetrated four miles into Bosche territory, a very respectable day's advance for warfare in France. Up to this point, the biggest brake on our momentum was prisoners.

Dozens of Fritzes, some practically children incongruous in their big steel helmets, stepped into view. Whether we yelled "Stick 'em up," or "Hände hoch!" they instantly surrendered.

The second team seemed to be manning this echelon of the Fritz defense. Certainly they were disordered, debris all around rudimentary trenches … empty ammo cartons, uniform rags, shattered ration carts, a German stovepipe boot containing half a leg.

I detailed Andy to gather some of our walking wounded as guards to take the POWs to the rear.

We kept pushing. Unfortunately, thanks to artillery hits and breakdowns, the tanks no longer were with us.

They could have helped in our assault against a little town named Missy-au-Bois.

Because of its name, I mentally commemorated the town to Missy, the French toddler we rescued. But without tanks, our speedy advance slowed drastically. A quick barrage of mortars and the fire of three machineguns from another ravine drove us to the ground.

Guardino and Johnson and I sheltered behind a low mound.

Johnson, once the fire-eater, lay on his side, knuckles to his teeth and knees pulled to his chin. He quivered in terror. "Are they gonna kill us?"

"Not if we stay put," Guardino said. He turned to me. "I think we're dealing with the first team now."

A burst of machinegun fire tore at our mound. "No shit," I said. "Definitely tougher troops. Time to think this over."

"You got any ideas?" he said.

"Not a damned one."

An instant later, we heard two grenades explode at what seemed to be the right distance and direction for the Bosche machinegun. I started to raise up to look. Guardino grabbed my shoulder. "What's the rush, Sarge? Somebody will let us know…"

I raised my head cautiously to see Harrison standing, firing a Chauchat toward the German position. Beside him, Crockett hurled another grenade. Both men dropped.

After the grenade blast, Crockett jumped up. "Got 'em! Got 'em!" He ran toward the German gun.

I also jumped up, I said, "Come on, Guardino, Johnson! Let's move."

I made out the outlines of the German gun's water jacket. The weapon sat on its mount amid clusters of field stone some farmer had dumped ages before.

Somebody appeared behind the gun, swinging it toward us. I aimed and shot. My bullet slammed through the front of his helmet, snapping the man's head back. He fell from sight and his weight tilted the gun barrel to the sky. Crockett jumped into the emplacement swinging his rifle like a dervish, killing gunners with his rifle butt and bayonet. Just as Gardino and I reached him, a chorus of evil little birds zipped past me, knocking Crockett flat. I heard the machinegun's rattle but couldn't see it.

"For Christ's sake, Sarge, get down!" I dropped back into our shelter.

"Where's that gun?" Somebody called that it was to the left. Didn't matter. They had us pinned down stopped.

It didn't look like we'd cut the road to Chateau-Thierry today.

Chapter 40
Winning – July 1918

I fumed, hoping the artillery's forward observers would spot the Bosche strongpoints and call in fire on them. I certainly wasn't going to send a runner through that curtain of machinegun fire.

Meanwhile Guardino spoke in quiet tones to Johnson. "Just compose yourself, Woody. We're safe enough here. And, hey, where's your rifle?"

"Not sure," Johnson said. "Think I lost it back thataway."

"Well, you can't be in combat without your rifle. So where do you think it is?"

"I don't know, but I'm not going out there to look for it. Not now, I'm not."

Just then came a rattle, thump and rush. Little Zimmer did a baseball slide into our rocky shelter. "Phew," he said. "Kinda busy out there."

He was carrying two rifles.

"Johnson," he said, "I think this might be your Enfield."

"No it's not. I don't want it," Johnson said.

Zimmer smirked and turned to me.

"Sergeant," he said, "there's a little notch behind you in this rockpile and a pretty good screen of brush. If you trade me positions, I think I could pick off those gunners."

Johnson practically screamed, "Don't let him do it, Sarge! It'll draw their attention. They'll kill us all."

Guardino yanked out his bayonet and placed its point against Johnson's neck. "You just got *my* attention, Woody," he snarled. "Not another damned word or I'll slit you ear to ear. Got it?"

In a series of nervous jerks Johnson nodded his head.

"Okay, Harry," I said, "that's enough. Put your pig-sticker away." Guardino gave me a black look, but sheathed his bayonet.

Thinking it would help Johnson to be occupied, I said "Look, this position is too small for four of us. So, Johnson, I don't care what you use or how you do it, but start digging this hole deeper. Right now."

"But I don't have a shovel or any…"

"I don't care, Johnson. Use your fingernails. Or your helmet. Or you John Thomas, or the tripod of that German machinegun. Start digging. Now!"

I traded positions with Zimmer. He propped his other rifle into narrow notch between two pieces of field stone. That's when I noticed it had a telescopic sight… and it surprised me to see the rifle was a German Mauser.

"Where the hell did you get that?"

"Off this Heinie sniper. He was dead, of course. So I tried a couple of shots with it and liked it real well. Near as I could judge it's real accurate at five hundred yards. So maybe I can get that machinegun crew. They ain't that far off."

"Have at it," I said. "Those boys been holding us up."

Zimmer carefully eased the rifle into its notch. He reached out to break two branches from the brush screen.

"Here goes," he said.

I swear Zimmer was so small that when he fired, the kick seemed to jerk his upper body about a foot to the rear.

"Got one," he whispered. He cocked the bolt. "I like this Mauser," he murmured as he settled his sight on its next victim. "It's a Model '98 so that it cocks when you open the bolt. It makes for a lot smoother …"

Crack!

"… action than the Enfield. That's two. Those Huns sure are looking around now. Seem kind of worried."

Crack!

"Shit! I missed! But at least I'm keeping 'em busy. They ain't firing right now. So some other folks are shooting at them."

While Johnson scraped pathetically at stony earth beneath us, Zimmer killed two more gunners. I joined him firing at the German Maxim crew, noting that my Springfield had a lighter bark than his Mauser.

Either firearm did the job which, basically, was to halt that machinegun and let us move to the east again.

As Zimmer and I got out of the hole, Guardino told Johnson. "That's enough digging. Grab your rifle and come with us."

He did. Meanwhile, squad by squad, Company B began appearing out of the ground and trotting east.

Within a minute, most of us dropped back to earth as two more machineguns began firing. But once down, we crawled forward – even Johnson came with us – rising and shooting at the gunners when their attention was divided.

The gunners' fire cut into us. I got to thinking that the casualty ratio was about even. It seemed that each time we took out an eight-man Bosche machinegun nest, it cost us nearly eight Yank casualties.

The balance seem to swing to the Huns when they got their mortars working again. A rifleman can't do much about that except go flat.

We all were hugging momma earth when a flight of Spads started attacking the mortar positions. Somebody at headquarters must have been on the phone with the nearest airdrome. The little planes repeatedly swooped down toward the German positions, their dual machineguns chattering.

I yelled at the top of my lungs, "Come on! They've cut down the mortar fire. Let's move while we can."

Men arose from the ground and began racing east with us. One plane crashed in front of us. The pilot broke his way out of the wreckage, a pile of broken sticks and wadded canvas. We thanked him and sent him limping west with a small batch of prisoners.

Company B went through the same exercise four more times, either taking out Hun positions or waiting for artillery or the airmen to do it for us.

By 1600 hours, the few of us surviving actually came within view of Soisson's church steeples. We hadn't advanced far enough to cross the highway or railroad line, but because we'd penetrated six miles into Bosche territory so that our artillery now could register on both arteries.

As it turned out, that threat did the job.

Right around dusk, a series of enormous explosions erupted to the south. By nightfall, the southern horizon glowed red. The Bosche were burning their supplies

"Battalion reports they'll send us reinforcements tonight," I said, "so we can attack tomorrow."

I also hoped headquarters would bless us a new skipper and executive officer.

I'm happy to say we didn't attack.

The next morning, July 22, I was swamped with getting our troops supplied for a new attack and loading our company's wounded aboard the empty trucks.

In the midst of that, a group of kilted Scottish officers presented themselves to me.

"Sergeant, we oonderstand ye command this company."

"Right. What about it?"

"We've coom to relieve ye. You and your men have earned a hell of a rest. The 15th Scottish Division is taking over from the First Yank Division."

"What?"

"Right. We're part of three corps attacking all along the line from here to Chateau-Thierry. We're going to drive the Huns east from the Marne to the Aisne."

I saluted them. "Gentlemen, you are welcome."

Chapter 41

A Long Pause – July 1918

When I reported to battalion asking for a new commander, a snooty three-stripe paper-pusher said no company grade officers were available. He told me casualties among lieutenants and captains had been heavy.

I stared at him.

"Yeah, Mr. Clerk, in case you haven't heard losses among enlisted people have been a bit heavy, too. Fact is, we could use someone like you up on the line." He turned pink.

Stepping outside, I leaned against a tree. "Great! Just great! Now what?" I almost fell asleep mulling what to do.

Then I spotted Major Creek and half-stumbled over to him to plead our case. After saluting, I said, "Sir, we don't have *any* officers in Company B now. And I'm sure not qualified to run a company …"

"Whoa, Sergeant," the major said. "You look worse than a singed cat! Join me in my tent and take a breather."

Once at his field desk in the tent, he told me to take a seat. "Sergeant, you and I have served together since when?"

"That would be 1909 at Jefferson Barracks, Sir."

"Right, going on ten years. And Max, right now you look a bit frazzled. Maybe you could use a drink."

"Sir, I sure wouldn't turn one down."

He grinned and brought two small glasses out of the desk and opened a dark ornate bottle.

"The US Army doesn't provide hard liquor to its rank and file," he said as he poured, "but here's some war booty -- captured Danzig Goldwasser. I'm sure some of your boys have liberated

Bosche booze, so here's part of your share. Oh, by the way, I recommend chugging it rather than sipping."

We both chugged it. I had to fight to resume normal breathing. "Wow, sir! That's wicked stuff!"

He chuckled and then turned to business.

"Sergeant, we've ordered four lieutenants and a captain for Company B, but at the moment we're fresh out. So you'll have to carry on for a bit."

"Yessir," I said. He tilted the bottle toward me and I extended my glass for a refill.

"By the way," he said, "you did a hell of a fine job with the company. I'm recommending you for a decoration. Now for a time you and your men will get a well-earned rest while you refit and make up your losses."

"Yessir, that means a lot of making up. I haven't got the butcher bill with me, but in size right now, Company B looks more like a reinforced platoon than a company."

He gave me a grim look. "Yeah, our butcher bill is very high. It's preliminary, but it looks like First Division lost close to seven thousand killed and wounded."

"Jesus!"

"Exactly," he said. "But on the other hand, we captured about four thousand Bosche and seventy-some of their field guns.

"We and Second Division paid the price of breaking that supply line.

"Now others like the Frogs and the Scots will force the Bosche away from the Marne. But we'll need you to get your new people trained and ready. The Huns aren't going back to Germany…" he paused and chugged his drink.

I did the same, coughed, and sputtered, "*Whew*! Not 'til we drive them back, right?"

"Exactly," he replied. "The Bosche absolutely will not skedaddle. It'll be a fighting withdrawal every step of the way.

"They'll buy time for their engineers to fortify defensive positions along the Aisne-Vesel line. Trenches, bunkers and even concrete pillboxes. It'll be just as tough as anything we've encountered heretofore."

He paused. "Headquarters is predicting that it'll be 1919 before they cave in.

"So, Max, go on back to your boys. Promote the ones you can trust and use them to train replacements. One of the reasons we lost so many officers was that they had to lead fairly green troops.

"Well, after what they've been through this past week, your boys aren't green. They're veterans. They'll help wise up the newcomers to survival in combat. The replacements should start arriving soon. We're going to need Company B again."

"When does it look like you'll have some officers assigned to us, sir?"

"I can't guess how soon you'll get them but I'll make sure yours know enough to pay attention to their first sergeant."

I stood up and saluted. "Thanks for the drink, sir. With your permission, I'll now stagger back to my temporary command."

# # #

Roll call revealed that of an original strength of 162 men and officers, we now had no officers and 93 men. I appointed Guardino, Zimmer, DeVries and Martinez temporary platoon commanders.

Adamczak was to be a training NCO and Andy Hart would be my exec. Their first duty was to get me a list of lost and damaged equipment.

Then I took up a job I absolutely hated – writing letters to the surviving relatives. What tortured me was the certainty that no matter what I wrote or how well I put it, my words wouldn't do a damn thing to ease the pain or suffering.

All too often I hadn't known the dead man well enough to make the letter personal… to reflect on his sense of humor or his ability to scrounge. The letters needed something better than "The War Department regrets to inform you…yadda, yadda, yadda."

I found two men with beautiful penmanship. So I drafted the letters and they penned the final versions. "God," I thought to myself as I drafted the forty-third letter, "no wonder officers have such lousy tempers."

When I dropped off a batch of letters to the regimental post office I spotted the first batch still sitting there after three days. "Goddammit, why haven't you sent off those letters? Who the hell runs this show? I'm not kidding. Who's in charge?"

At that point a very cold voice behind me said, "What's the problem here?"

"The problem," I said as I turned, "is that some so-called officer here has his head up his..." only to discover I was addressing General Pershing looking frosty as Chicago's winter wind. I kept yammering.

"Sorry, general, but I'm in temporary command of a rifle company with a hell of a lot of casualties. I've worked till all hours writing letters to the families and then I discover the letters still sitting here rather than being sent to St. Nizaire."

"Why are *you* writing the letters, Sergeant?"

"Because there's no one else to do it!"

He looked up from me to the postal clerk, "Who's in charge?"

"Uh, sir, it's Captain Evanston, sir."

"Get him. Now!"

"Sir, he's in the officers' mess..."

"*Now!*"

"Yessir!" The clerk bolted from his office.

The general turned back to me. "Sergeant, thank you. I can take it from here. We'll see that your mail is headed to the ship today."

"Yessir! Thank you sir!" I saluted and left.

Chapter 42

Resting − August 1918

As I drafted my final letter, Major Creek pulled back the flap of my tent.

I jumped to attention but the major said, "At ease, Sergeant Colemen. I want to introduce your new commanding officer, Captain Howard Felton."

I started to salute but the captain thrust his hand toward me. "Put her there, Top."

As we shook hands, I said, "Welcome, sir. Glad to have you here. We need you."

He gave a big smile. "Oh, probably not as much as I'll need you and your old hands. We'll be getting some new lieutenants soon and we'll have to show them the ropes."

The captain was very erect and correct, but didn't seem to possess the put-you-in-your-place impulse found in so many new officers. At least he seemed willing to learn first whether the other NCOs and I were competent.

We visited the sergeants who temporarily commanded our platoons. When we returned to my office – sorry, his office – he started skimming the men's files plus medical reports about which of the wounded could come back, and when.

I told him I felt we could rely on all the platoons' temporary commanders, but that I was especially impressed with Zimmer.

"He's brand new with us," I said. "But he's very cool and self-possessed in combat and I think he'd be an excellent leader. I'd recommend keeping an eye on him, sir."

"Thanks, Max, I'll keep that in mind. Meanwhile, what's the situation with our gear?"

# # #

Once we dived into our paperwork, I came to like the new skipper.

"God, I hate paper-shuffling," he told me once. "But it's a goddamned means to the end which is a fighting-ready company of infantry. So we've got to propitiate the bureaucratic gods at Chaumont or otherwise…"

"Not quite sure what that means, sir," I said, "except that maybe we could run out of bullets at a real embarrassing time."

He nodded. "Exactly."

Captain Felton, an ROTC graduate, was from a wheat-growing family in eastern Colorado. He'd done a stint as a lieutenant in Haiti and, when the war began, was transferred to a training battalion in Michigan.

"So when they gave me my railroad tracks, I applied for a transfer to the AEF," he said. "Once I got here, they put me to work with General Harbord to expedite unloading time at the ports."

"I bet that was interesting, sir."

"About like watching wheat grow," he said. "But the general did get things organized pretty quickly, so that we now are bringing ten thousand Yanks a day into France. Then I applied for a transfer to First Division and here I am."

Within a week we received twelve returning wounded and a pair of first lieutenants. Lieutenant Schreiber was big enough to fight heavyweight. Lieutenant Graham was short, skinny, chinless and pimply-faced.

He surprised us all because he seemed to be a natural leader.

When one of the men muttered that he looked like a tissey-prissle, the lieutenant snapped, "What's your name, soldier?"

Red-faced, the man said, "Michaels, sir."

"Well, Michaels! To you, it's *Lieutenant* Tissy Prissle."

"But, Michaels," he went on, "my Mom really prefers that you use my family name. And you *don't* want my Momma mad at you!"

The men laughed and relaxed. I could read their minds: *Hey, this guy's okay.*

Even Michaels grinned. He saluted, "I'm sorry, sir. Won't happen again. Please tell Mrs. Graham I apologize."

Minutes later, criticizing a man for having a dirty rifle, he made it funny. "Your name's Onslow? Right? Onslow, ain't they warned you about loaning weapons to hogs? They cain't clean a rifle for doodley squat. So now you best do it yo'self."

He wound up the formation by giving Sergeant Zimmer instructions for the day. Then he just said "Carry on," and left Zimmer to it.

Schrieber, on the other hand, struck me as being a rank-conscious bully. He came down hard on two men – returning wounded who still limped. Then he blamed Sergeant DeVries, in front of his own men, for the two veterans' alleged slack attitude.

I had a word with Captain Felton about that. I wasn't present for the subsequent dressing-down, of course. But I did overhear the skipper bellow about the necessity for officers to uphold rather than demean their NCOs' authority. "Back up your sergeants, lieutenant, and they and the men'll watch your back. Otherwise in combat you could get real, *real* lonely. Get me?"

We received fifty green replacements straight from the states. The skipper welcomed them.

"You men are joining the finest fighting company in the best regiment of the best division, the Big Red One. I'm giving you an important order. Pay very, very close attention to your veteran comrades. As our granddaddies said back in the Civil War, these men have seen the elephant. They've *been* there! So heed their lessons. Learn from them and learn well. If you do, it'll markedly improve your chances of staying alive and getting home."

I distributed the new men among our platoons. I didn't need to tell anyone to start training them.

# # #

The captain had us start with some hard marches, several routes taking us across battered ground over which the armies had fought.

At the fifteen-mile mark on one of our hikes, I told Andy, "Looks like it kind of wakes up the new men."

"Yeah," he said, "it's not as worrisome as relieving the Blue Devils' trenches at night. But at least we've got the same smells that we did back then."

"Yeah, it's right pungent."

One of the new men marching behind me said, "Good God, I think I just saw a skull!"

"Where?"

"It was behind a bush. We just passed it."

"Yank, Frog or Hun?"

"Donno, sir."

Somebody else chimed in. "It's damned indecent to have us march among the dead. Somebody should have policed up this battleground."

I looked over my shoulder, "Who do you think should get that duty?"

"I don't know, Sarge. Maybe some service troops?"

"Service troops? Great idea! Hey, Sergeant Zimmer! Have a corporal break this particular squad out of the march and police up this area for, say, ten minutes. Then these service troops can bring up the rear of the company."

"Should they bury the remains?"

"Naah. Bring 'em along with any identity disks you find. We can turn it all over to Graves Registration."

Soon I snorted in amusement. The lad who said it was indecent to march here was getting a whispered vicious cussing from his buddies. "From now on, Jergins, keep your damned yap shut and your fucking opinions to yourself."

Chapter 43

Bonding – August 1918

About noon, Captain Feltman detailed me to escort our new lieutenants to Chaumont for a training program.

"Sir," I said, "I think it might be better if we left early tomorrow. There's bound to be some tie-ups with convoys this afternoon."

"No," he grinned. "Load 'em up now and take off. I think you can use the break. By the way, I made it clear to them that you're in charge. Neither you nor the driver is their servant. If you have to put up somewhere along the way, here's a wad of francs."

Our other two new officers were ROTC graduates – Tim Carney, Pennsylvania State, and Barton Rogers, University of Missouri. Rogers was a banty weight. Carney looked like a 6-5 mountain of muscle. Joining us as exec was Second Lieutenant Zimmerman

We hadn't been on the road ten minutes before Schreiber started yelling at the driver for hitting so many road cuts. Since the road was a virtual washboard, I was debating whether, as the man in charge, to tell my superior officer to shut his damned mouth.

Carney did it for me.

"Schreiber, you'd be wise to take it easy on your fellow soldier who's…"

"Fellow soldier, my ass," Schreiber said. "He's just a damn private."

Speaking quietly, Carney said, "Look, lieutenant, we depend on this private – who is our comrade in arms -- to deliver us safely to Chaumont. Being as how you and I will have to work together in the months ahead as comrades in arms against a very tough and determined enemy, you'd best simmer down. Otherwise you've got another tough determined enemy sitting right here in this truck."

"Two enemies," Rogers said.

"Make it three," Graham added.

"No, it's four," Zimmerman said.

The drive became very quiet except for the jouncing and banging on the road.

When a particularly hard bump made the truck interior resound like a trash barrel, Rogers tried to lighten the mood. "Any of you fellas ever hear the German word for 'rattletrap?' I think it's much more descriptive."

Schreiber, who seemed eager for a change in subject, said, "No, what's the word?"

"It's *Klapperkasten*."

"Oh, ho! That's rich," the driver laughed. "Makes it sound like you're right inside this here truck."

"So what's this training that we're headed for?" Graham asked. The four of them began speculating about problems that caused them the greatest difficulty in their brief military careers.

As I predicted, traffic was bad. MPs stopped us at a crossroads for two long convoys. By the time we arrived in Tours it was 2000 hours. I directed the driver to a three-story hotel and paid for three rooms.

The officers dined separately from us and I could see it was a tense meal. Graham and Rogers tried to keep conversation going, but Schreiber and Carney silently eyed each other.

The hotel manager spoke to the officers and they directed him to me.

"Monsieur," he said, "each night at precisely 24 of the clock, the Bosche avion fly over to drop bombs in Tours. We invite our guests therefore to come to the abri."

"Abri?"

Rogers turned from his table to us. "They have a shelter in the basement. He wants a supplement to the room fee to cover the cost of champagne that they serve during the bombing raids."

"Oui," the manager grinned. "Only ten more franc per guest."

I asked, "What if it's cloudy and the Bosche don't come?"

Pained at such a boorish question, the manager said he'd refund the supplement.

"You will tell us if the Bosche are coming?"

"Oh, oui, sir. Bien sur. We give alarm."

# # #

It was cloudy when I turned in at 2200 hours. The sirens began wailing at 2330. The sky had cleared. A big flight of planes was droning our way.

The driver and I pulled on our gear and joined the lieutenants and other guests processing down the stairways.

The basement surprised us. Not a dank place, but two large luxuriously carpeted rooms. Rather than stone, the walls were paneled and decorated with paintings.

Several of the guests were attractive, too. One, a tall brunette, fluttered her eyes at Carney. A tiny blonde told our driver in very poor but delightfully-accented English that she needed support because the Bosche terrified her.

When waiters began opening champagne, Schreiber sat down at the piano and suggested that we entertain our French friends and hosts with some good old American folk singing.

We crooned *Home On The Range* and *Old Kentucky Home,* receiving (I thought) undeserved applause plus several feminine calls of *Encore! Encore!*

We worked our way through *Old MacDonald Had A Farm* and half-way through *She'll Be Comin' Round The Mountain* when we heard distant thumping – bombs and antiaircraft fire.

The lights went out, eliciting several feminine screams. I judged them to be less than full panic but definitely designed to solicit protective hugs plus kisses. The staff lit candles and Schreiber continued his concert.

I got the bright idea to try a jaunty French language camp song, *Alloutte*. The suggestion made me a hero with my comrades.

See, I didn't know French and so I didn't realize *Alloutte* is no mere camp song. It's a series of verses each calling for progressive removal of plumage from a lark, starting at the head -- *Je te plumerai la tête* -- and working down.

The crowd sang a good many rounds of the song. Some of the candles burned out so it was difficult to tell in semi-darkness, but I had the impression considerable plumage was coming off. Schreiber's performance at the piano began to falter and then stopped altogether.

# # #

Outdoors next morning, Lieutenant Rogers and I examined the miniscule bomb damage. The weapons apparently weighed less than twenty pounds. They did little more than interrupt sleep...and give excuses for parties.

As we looked about, the lieutenant genially described to me the concept of double entendre. "That's why some ladies in that shelter entered enthusiastically into the spirit of *Alloutte*. I suspect some of them are chippies and more or less permanent residents at the hotel."

"Chippies?"

"Yes, sergeant. Some folks refer to them as the Angels of the Night."

"Oh! Got it, sir."

Because we all suffered hangovers, we dubiously climbed into the truck very leery of the noisy slam-banging ride ahead.

But the party in the shelter seemed to have knit us closer together. When we congratulated Schreiber on his skill at the keyboard, he almost became friendly.

Maybe it's what the skipper had in mind.

Chapter 44

Refitting – August 1918

We didn't realize it at the time, of course, but the battle that Company B had helped fight in July was the opening round in the Kaiser's defeat.

Or Ludendorff's, if you prefer, since by then the glowering old son of a bitch virtually ran the German state.

As far as the company was concerned, though, it was time to lick our wounds, rest, refit and train our replacements for the battles ahead.

We found the process complicated. The old hands, united by searing combat and standing out in their ragged gear, ignored the freshly uniformed arrivals from the states. In fact, they seemed contemptuous of new arrivals, leaving them confused outsiders.

Our lieutenants, also new, seemed unaware of the replacements' feeling of isolation.

Captain Felton and I teamed up. He lowered the boom on his officers. I came down hard on the sergeants.

"These kids may be fresh fish," I told Guardino, "but you better get your boys to welcome them. Make them feel at home."

"Shit, Max, it ain't worth it. These recruits are so damned dumb and green."

"Oh? You *weren't* dumb and green when you got off the boat? Look, Harry, the Bosche killed or chopped up a lot of us because we had no idea of how to fight. Well, these kids can shoot and throw grenades. And if you show them when and where they'll do alright. You need to show them how a low mound in the earth can be great cover. They can save your damned life if you guide them and make them part of your squads."

He nodded. "Okay. I see what you mean."

"Good! Make damned sure your vets welcome them for real! Otherwise they'll just be more fertilizer for these French wheat fields …and you, too, my friend, if they don't know how to cover your back!"

# # #

I was overlooking one of Adamczak's training classes which took place to a distant undercurrent -- combat rumbling far off as hundreds of thousands of Yanks, Tommies and Poilus pushed Hun armies back northeast.

Toward the end of the class, a replacement, a willowy sensitive-looking kid, held up a hand. "I just can't understand something."

Adamczak said, "What can't you understand, Cramer? You pull the pin. That releases the spoon which frees the hammer to snap down onto the fuse. The fuse ignites and so you better throw the grenade before it explodes."

"Sorry, sarge. I know all that. I just can't understand the Germans."

Another trainee growled, "Awww, jeeeze! Here we go again!"

Cramer continued solemnly. "Germans have taken science, art and literature and music to their highest forms. Yet never has a nation devoted so much talent to such god awful butchery. The bastards just destroy everything. And then they booby trap the rubble that's left. I just don't get it."

Adamczak took a deep breath.

"Good point, Cramer," he said. "That's Germans for you."

"You mentioned music. So, look at Beethoven. It took him more than two years to compose his ninth symphony. He hand-wrote every damned note of a different score for each instrument of a full orchestra plus the music for a gigantic choir of men and women with voices ranging from bass to soprano.

"Cramer, he didn't just compose that symphony, he made it goddamned perfect. I had one professor tell me you can't add or subtract a single note without ruining the entire thing.

"And the onery old bastard did it all while being as deaf as a post!"

Somebody asked, "So what?"

"So what? Here's what! He was German. That's Germans for you. Whatever they turn to, they go at it like they're killing snakes. They're driven, methodical, exacting and fanatical. They're perfectionists.

"And their army brings that same intensive methodical drive to combat. They fight in step with mortars, artillery, gas and even aeroplanes.

"First they machinegun your position, keeping your head down as their riflemen work close in. Then the riflemen throw those stick grenades into your trench. So you're either forced to retreat, and maybe get shot in the back, or you surrender."

I interrupted. "You men have heard what the Limies say?"

"What, sarge?"

"The British, as you know, are damned tough soldiers, but they have this saying: 'You don't know war until you've fought Germans'."

The kids went a little wide in the eyes.

"But look," Adamczak said, "we can thank God they're not all geniuses like Beethoven. Besides, we ain't in the music business. We don't fight to entertain a theater full of listeners. We fight to kill Germans and we Yanks have a big advantage over them."

"What's that, Sarge?"

"It's inside American noggins. You guys rile me because you always want to know 'Why?' 'Why this' and 'Why that' until I'm ready for them to put me in a padded cell and throw away the key.

"But that's the thing about us Yanks. When we tangle with Huns, our brains go into action. I think most German soldiers are so disciplined they have no time for thinking. So when the Hun gets in a bind, it can stop him cold."

Adamczak stopped and laughed.

"You boys know what happens to every German recruit the minute he gets into uniform? He and his comrades are ordered to line up with their rifles out on the muddy parade ground and the sergeant yells, 'Verrüken!' And a second later, 'Liegen'!

"That means 'Advance!' and then 'Lie down!' And for hour after hour they do it just like that. Stand up! Advance! Take cover. Stand up! Advance! Take cover…and so on. It's like training dogs.

"In the USofA," Adamczak said, "we taught you 'Attention' and 'At Ease' and how to salute. And then it's do lots of push-ups and head on to the rifle range."

"Don't forget peeling spuds, Sarge."

"Yeah, okay, wiseass! But you get my point. By the way, do you know what our motto is in the US Army infantry?"

"What, Sarge?"

"Do *something* even if it's wrong."

He glanced at his watch.

"And now I see you got me to bullshitting past the end of class. Form up! Cramer, march 'em over to Guardino's station. And I want to hear you calling cadence."

Chapter 45

Settling Down – August 1918

Within three weeks, I got the impression that the replacements were starting to feel a bit more at home within our company.

You'd sense it of an evening when walking among the tents or past the barns.

You'd see a group outside a tent – some in new uniforms, others in old – and hear them laughing; not just one guy chuckling, but maybe five people doubling over in a roaring belly laugh.

I told the platoon sergeants they'd done a good job in fitting the new people in.

"Well, it wasn't us entirely," Guardino said.

"Nope," Adamczak added. "It was the discovery that these French farms don't just make vin plonk. Nossir, they also brew some pretty damned good beer. And it's cheap."

DeVries nodded. "That's all true.

"But the other thing is that these kids brought some fresh jokes from the states with them. And then some of them are real showmen who brought a song with them. It's from some New York musical about us Doughboys and I think it's called 'Over There'."

"Yeah," Guardino added. "This one kid got hisself oiled with four or five beers and sang the thing through for his squad. As he pretended to march himself off stage he was waggling his helmet instead of a top hat. Pretty soon people started showing up from other squads."

"Sure beats that other song," Andy told me.

"What song?"

"Oh, it's a real funeral march. The old troops started it when they were in the line. They were just singing 'We're here because we're here because we're here…' and it just keeps going like that. Really puts you in the dumps."

I proposed to Captain Felton that we invite talented people in the company to set up a musical show of some sort.

"Well, hell, sergeant why just the company?" he said. "Let's think big about this. What about a talent show or our own vaudeville? Maybe the battalion would help sponsor it."

Major Creek bought the idea at once.

The 16th had a regimental band, of course.

But before long we learned that many of the new troop – I still thought of them as uniformed civilians – also were pretty fair musicians.

Lieutenant Schreiber became the organizer. I guess you'd call him the producer and director. Anyhow, we wound up with what you'd call a vaudeville comic opera.

Schreiber himself played a pretty mean honky-tonk piano between acts.

A huge corporal from third battalion lifted the front end of a truck off the stage – motor and all. He held it for thirty seconds, and then put it down, put on a set of straps and towed it off stage.

Guardino bellowed out *O Sole Mio* to thunderous applause. Clapping was merely polite when Sergeant Zimmer attempted the tenor opening of Beethoven's Ninth, whatever that was.

A stand-up comic produced roars of laughter claiming to be a Jewish Catholic who always took a lawyer when going to confession.

Adamzcak gave a scholarly lecture explaining to the doughboys that vaudeville got its start in France in the 1880s. Then it migrated through Canada to the United States.

One more act came on, a very pretty female impersonator trying to sing a love song.

I expected some wild cheering when, for the finale, the band started playing *Stars And Stripes Forever*.

I never found out what caused it, but half-way through the performance a fight broke out in the audience. It spread rapidly until we had a virtual riot on our hands.

With the aid of MPs, senior NCOs and some officers we managed to quell the brawl.

The police arrested fifteen men, mostly from our battalion.

Next morning I went to the stockade to see the prisoners who were from my company. The stockade was the ground floor of a barn. I recognized Andrews in a horse stall standing over Crockett who still was nursing his two bullet wounds.

The prisoners were a sight.

Andrews had a gorgeous black eye and a fat lower lip. Assorted cuts and scrapes decorated the other troops' faces. Each man ached to tell his side of the story.

"So, you guys, what the hell happened?"

All fifteen started to reply simultaneously, giving loud and sincere allegations about drunkenness, pick-pocketing, nasty comments about the female impersonator and some MP bully with a truncheon trying to clobber poor wounded Crockett.

"Shut up!" I snapped. "All of you!"

The funny thing was that about half of them were in new uniforms and the others were obvious veterans…and all seemed to be getting along.

I asked a veteran, an old El Paso acquaintance, what he thought of the fresh-faced kid beside him.

"Hell, sarge, Charley here is a real hombre! Ain't so hot with his fists, but he sure tossed a couple of those third battalion bastards right onto their keesters."

As he spoke, a lot of vigorous nodding took place among the prisoners.

"Well, shame on you sorry bastards," I said. "I'd say you're all candidates for a court martial. I guess I'll go see what the judge advocate has in store for you."

They looked pretty glum as I left.

# # #

Instead of the JAG, I went to the orderly room to have a long chat with Captain Felton.

"Sir, I don't know what charges they'll bring against these jokers, but I think that brawl did wonders for morale.

"A lot of guys sometimes just gotta sock each other to become buddies. If the prisoners I talked to are any evidence, I think the show and the fight pulled these guys together."

"Sergeant Coleman, are you ragging me? Do you think this has helped in some strange way? Really?"

"Yessir, I do. I'm not bullshitting you. The fight got pretty wild, I grant you, but I don't think any real damage occurred … other than a few shiners and split lips."

"Mmm. You may be right, Top. But I don't know how higher headquarters feels. Some of those boxing matches kind of hustled the colonel away from his front row seat."

"I understand, sir. Well, maybe it don't make much sense, but I think the brawl helped make us a better fighting outfit."

"I hope so," the captain said. "Pretty soon here," he added, "we're going to need all the fight we can come up with."

"Can you tell me what's up, sir?"

"Keep it to yourself for now, Max. We have a briefing for officers and NCOs late today. We're going to assault the Wilhelm Line, the south face of the St. Mihiel salient."

"Just us, sir?"

"Oh hell, no. It's an all-American show. We're now officially part of the U.S. First Army and that army -- seven American divisions – is going to take on the Bosche quite soon.

# # #

In the dark I heard a nervous young voice direct a question to Andy.

"Sergeant Hart, how do we actually attack? I mean what do we really do?"

"Christ, Billings, we've gone over this. Remember? You move forward with your squad. You hug the barrage that the artillery fires in front of us. You keep moving until you meet resistance."

"We actually walk? Upright?"

"Yeah, Billings, upright. "

"So, what if the Germans start shooting?"

"There's no, 'if' Billings. It is *when* the Huns start to shoot. And that is when you take cover and return fire.

"Our automatic rifle and rifle sections will set up a base of fire. Rifle grenade sections fire at the enemy, too. Grenadiers move far enough forward to throw their hand grenades, all making the enemy's life hell."

"You make it sound simple, sarge."

"Well, it is simple. It's also very noisy.

"But after a while you get used to it…a little bit, anyway." He slapped Billings' shoulder. "Look, the main thing is to watch the old hands. Do as they do and do as they tell you. You'll do okay, son."

Chapter 46

On The Offensive – September 1918

Waiting and pacing in the trenches before first light September 12 was nail-biting hell, as always. A chilly drizzle didn't help, either.

It was good, though, to see the artillery shell flashes dance throughout the Germans' Wilhelm Line – the defensive belt of wire and trenches we had to assault and cross.

"Not much help there," Adamczak said. "That shelling won't do a thing except spoil the Huns' morning coffee. They're going to be spitting mad about it."

"Jesus, Bill, do you have to be such a spoil sport?"

"Max, what do you expect? I'm a realist. After barrages I've seen them drag those MGs out of their holes and start shooting as if nothing happened."

"And holes there are aplenty," Lieutenant Zimmerman said. "They showed us some pictures taken from aeroplanes, and it looks like for a mile or two it's just a damned checkerboard of holes forty or fifty feet apart, all connected by trenches. Loads of cover for them."

I started to reply, "Yeah, well…." when the whistles called us to climb out of the trenches and over the top.

Almost immediately Adamczak's prediction seemed to come true. Despite the shelling, Fritz's typewriters began rattling. Bullets whizzed and whined around us like mosquitoes. Most of the fire seemed high, though, so we advanced at a crouch into the barbed wire.

"Lordy be!" Andy yelled. "Their wire's gone all crumbly. We can just break right through."

The Bosche had occupied this salient since invading France in 1914 so that much of their barbed wire had rusted to fragility. Enough barbs were left to snag puttees, pant legs and wrists and hands, but it was a nuisance more than an obstacle.

The fire from their trenches and MG pits was pointed and lethal as ever. The first two squads advancing across the shell-blasted ground took a few casualties.

Even so, our Chauchat gunners showed they knew their business. Fire spitting from the muzzles of those clumsy guns kept at least some Hun heads down while the grenade sections worked their way within throwing range.

I yelled to one grenadier. "Hey, watch what you're loading, stupid!" He had just slipped the grenade's steel rod down the bore of his Enfield. But instead of a blank, he was about to jack a regular cartridge into the action.

He gave a silly grin and chambered a blank round instead. He pulled the grenade's pin, tilted the rifle toward a Hun gun pit, and fired.

The grenade's arc looked to me to be too high, but it exploded perhaps five feet above the Bosche gunners. With rifle fire and Chauchats focused on them, the Huns went *hände noch*.

From my spot in first platoon, I saw our men systematically clean out other nodes of resistance.

It got to the point that some of our men simply slung their rifles while directing a good many prisoners to the rear.

"Looks to me like the Fritz command saw us coming and pulled some of their troops back," Captain Felton said. "It was the smart move."

"I certainly have no objection, sir."

The skipper and I were advancing together but keeping our five yard separation. Instead of a pistol, he carried an Enfield just like an ordinary rifleman.

"Why the rifle, sir?"

He snorted. "Camouflage, Max. I want Bosche snipers to think I'm just one of the boys."

My next big worry – the whole regiment's big worry – was Montsec, a forested butte jutting twelve hundred feet above what otherwise was a gently rolling plain.

First Division was leading the main assault toward a little town named Viguenells. And we of the 16th Infantry, the division's left-hand regiment, were to pass tight against Montsec's east shoulder.

It looked as if the Bosche up there could subject us to plunging fire, not to mention calling heavy artillery strikes upon us.

We hugged the artillery barrage which advanced a hundred yards every three minutes. Meanwhile, a separate set of artillery blasted Montsec's wooded crest to splinters. After that, gunners dropped hundreds of smoke shells onto the hill, blinding the Bosche observers.

"For once," Captain Felton said, "things seem to be going according to plan."

We kept moving north and the German troops retired before us, some of them making it a fighting retreat. A squad in feldgrau uniforms would suddenly appear out of a trench or from behind farmhouse rubble.

Three would kneel to fire at us as the other five or six retreated and took cover. Then the trio leapfrogged past their buddies who took over firing at us.

"Gotta admire them," the captain told me. "A fighting retreat is the toughest thing you can ask of troops. Even when they want to flee, hey're keeping good order."

Our advance slowed when the lead squad came to the high banks of a creek.

Andy sent a runner to us. "There's four Hun machine guns covering the ground from beyond rifle grenade range. Sarge says we're going to try to flank them, but it might take time."

Lieutenant Zimmerman came trotting up from behind us. "We've got it handled," he said. "Go tell Sergeant Hart that a mortar section is setting up. Right quick here, we're gonna put a little salt on those birds' tail. After that his boys should be able to cross."

A few minutes later we heard *Thonk! Thonk!* The first mortar shell exploded far short of the target, in the creek itself. The second landed just beyond one of the enemy machinegun pits.

Having the range, the mortars spent ten minutes working over the Bosche positions. Coal-black explosions soon shrouded the target and Lieutenant Zimmerman waved his platoon across the creek and up the far bank.

We heard several grenades thump and with them a flurry of machinegun fire. Lowering his binoculars, the captain said, "Can't see a thing for the smoke. Let's move forward."

# # #

Lieutenant Zimmerman reported. "One of my grenadiers is dead and four of my people are wounded. Those damned machinegun crews just flat refused to give up. Damned fools fought to the last man."

I looked into the nearest machinegun pit. Eight bloodied Germans lay there.

Andy said, "Kind of a crazy picture ain't it?"

I said, "What do you mean?"

"Well, those big helmets of theirs look like heavy armor. You know, like those old Roman fighters wore."

"The gladiators?"

"Yeah, right. But look at those corpses. They're scrawny. Their belts are cinched way, way in. These boys ain't been feeding real well."

By 1300 hours we reached our day's objective, well in advance of our schedule, and were ordered to keep pushing.

We kept advancing against slowly stiffening resistance. At 1600 hours, we stopped for the day. Sergeant Zimmer was up marching about applauding his troops. "You boys did a hell of a great job today! We lost some buddies, but there's a story making the round that might make you feel better.

"Seems some quartermaster shavetail leading an ammo train got lost and run into a couple of squads of Bosche. He figured he was a dead man, but all they wanted to do was surrender to him.

Even their officers. They'd had enough of you First Division bastards. Boys, I think the German army is beginning to break."

The German soldiers never quit. But two months later – after a hell of a lot more people on both sides died -- the German leadership broke.

# # #

I spent the evening checking on casualties and making sure we had enough ammo, food and water for tomorrow. It was midnight when I reported back to the skipper.

After giving the report I couldn't help wondering how the kid with the question about Germans, Private Billings, was faring. He seemed so young and dumb.

"Well, by now," I muttered, "he's dead or all grown up."

"What's that?" the captain asked.

"Nothing, sir. Just thinking about one of the kids."

"Keep an eye on all of 'em," he said.

"Yessir. I'll try."

Chapter 47
Still Attacking – August 1918

Company B moved out next morning, meeting resistance that was tough in some spots.

Artillery still thumped and thudded in the distance. We heard occasional crackles of rifle and machinegun fire. But the day was fairly clear of battle dust and smoke.

"Fritz is stubborn here and there," Captain Felton said, "but even our green troops are learning how to handle it. The main thing is that he's either faltering or retreating."

"Easy to say," I thought, as our little headquarters group passed a German bunker now serving as a Yank aid station.

Most of the wounded were tight-lipped, but one corporal with a butchered leg tossed and writhed on the bunker floor. "Christ almighty," he groaned through gritted teeth, "can't you give me somethin' for the pain?"

We moved on quickly, following our platoons.

"Maybe it's wishful thinking," Corporal Anderson said, "but it does look like maybe the Fritzes are pulling out. I keep thinking they'll counterattack, but it just ain't happening…so far anyways."

"Wishful thinking, Charlie," I told the signalman, "I'll believe they quit when I see it."

"Corporal," the captain added, "I share your impression. But just stick to writing times and facts in the headquarters log. No wishful thoughts."

"Right, sir," the little clerk said.

A runner came pounding to us. I winced when he saluted the captain – sure proof to Bosche snipers about which of us was the skipper. But the captain didn't seem to worry and no sniper seemed to aim this way.

"What's up, son?"

"Cap'n, Lieutenant Graham wants you to know that we got us a squad into Viggles and that they made contact with a patrol from 28th Infantry. He wants permission to push on into town."

"Did you say Viggles?"

"Sorry, sir." The runner pulled out a piece of paper and handed it to captain. "I don't know how to say it right."

The captain glanced at the note. "Hot damn! We've got Vigneulles! Right according to plan, Very good. My compliments to the lieutenant. Tell him to stop in place and keep an eye peeled to the east. The Bosche still could counterattack so the rest of B Company will close up on his right."

He gave a big grin. "Seizing Vigneulles," he said. "A classic pincer attack -- the 28th assaulting from the west and us driving up from the south. Now we control a key crossroads that the Fritzes need. We've cut a lot of them off.""

By 1300 hours, we still heard artillery, but fighting stopped in our area. Our troops were walking with their rifles slung. Meanwhile, entire squads of Fritzes were coming to us, disarmed, hands up and helmets off.

The skipper waved me over. "Top, we're crawling with prisoners, so get some guards together and head them to the nearest French forces."

I found five walking wounded, among them a corporal. Just as I began giving them orders, a Fritz officer walked up to me.

I turned to meet him and he stiffened and clicked his heels. "Please forgive my bad English. You are control here?" He stood rigid as a ramrod, peering just left of my face.

"Yes, I'm in charge. What do you want?"

"Ah, ja. 'In charge,' you say. Yes, so, I am *kapitan*. I wish to surrender but to officer, not sergeant."

"Oh, for Christ's sake…" I stared back at him for a second. "Hell! Wait here, sir!"

In two minutes I returned with Lieutenant Schreiber. "Sir, this captain wishes to surrender to an officer I guess so he'll feel like it's official or something."

With that, I saluted both the Yank and Bosche officers. Both returned my salute very correctly and I did a sharp about face to return to my guard detail.

"Look," I told the guards, "I don't think these guys have any fight left in them. Keep your weapons handy, of course. Locked and loaded. But just hike the bastards to the nearest Frog outfit. Then find a dispensary to get yourselves treated."

"Got it, Top."

Schreiber called to me, so I marched back to him and saluted.

Trying to keep a straight face, he said, "Sergeant Coleman, you've met Captain Johann Eisenbeiss of the German Imperial Army."

I nodded to the captain. "Of course. Sir!"

Lieutenant Schreiber told me, "*Herr hauptman* Eisenbeis has formally surrendered himself and all these troops …"

The German captain interrupted, "*Ja, Einhundertzwanzig Gefangene.*"

"Yes, a hundred twenty prisoners. He will command the prisoners to cooperate fully with your guards and he asks only that they be marched out of this combat zone as soon as possible. Many of them are sick and they're all about half-starved.

"He has selected this other man, Sergeant Oltoff, to work with your guards."

"Very good, sir," I said.

The captain nodded to the sergeant who right-faced and barked out. "Achtung!"

The rather dispirited-looking Fritzes jumped to attention. The captain spoke to them briefly. Then the sergeant ordered them into a column of fours.

The captain said to me, "We are ready Sergeant."

"Thank you, sir. Okay, guys, move 'em out!"

Sergeant Olthoff called, "*Vorvärts marsch*!" and off they marched in perfect step.

I turned to the lieutenant. "Damned strange people."

"They sure as hell are. I wish we could get Ludendorff to put 'em in line like that and march them straight back to Berlin."

# # #

Having captured Vigneulles, we and the 28th pivoted east with the rest of the American forces.

"Where we headed now, Cap'n?"

"We're pushing them straight east to the so-called Michel Line. This will clear the Bosche from the St. Mihiel salient. Our orders are to halt there."

"The Michel Line?"

"Yep, it's another damned series of entrenchments and I bet it will have fairly new fresh barbed wire. We can be sure the Fritzes retreating in front of us will go to ground there."

As I think about it today, we should have just kept attacking.

It would have been costly. But stopping in place was bloody, too. The orders halted us on fairly bare ground with a scattering of abandoned bunkers and machinegun pits. As we arrived, the Bosche started shelling us.

Men sought what cover they could. None of us had shovels, so that many of our troops had to use their helmets to scrape holes in the earth.

Hearing an incoming shell, Captain Feltman and his orderly dived into the shelter of a nearby bunker. I ran to join them but fortunately had too far to go.

A thunderclap slammed me five feet backwards like a rag doll. Half-stunned and deafened, I rolled over to look for my rifle and helmet. Black smoke billowed over the shattered bunker.

We found nought of captain or corporal. The blast killing them was only one of the hundreds of booby traps the retreating Bosche left in bunkers and rifle pits.

In a sergeants' confab next day, Guardino snarled about it. "Crummy sonsabitches," he said. "We kicked their butts fair and square and then they booby trapped everything. Fucking sore losers! Booby traps didn't make one particle of difference in the battle. They lost."

"Oh, it makes one big difference," Adamczak said. "It makes me boil. From here on out, I'm never giving any German an even break."

"Me neither," Zimmer said.

"Yeah," Guardino said, "and you're German."

"Bullshit!" Zimmer shot back.

"I'm a Yank."

Chapter 48

Launch Point – August 1918

Rest. Blessed rest. We didn't get any.

Don't get me wrong. The troops of the 16th Infantry had five whole days to guzzle beer, eat and try to sleep with their nightmares. Some of the officers also got a couple of days off.

But us NCOs – we who run the Army day-to-day – got no rest. Period. For one thing, my job as B Company's first sergeant was to help our new skipper get to know his brand new command.

"But," as Captain Blackmun told me, shaking his head, "you and I don't have much time for that. I'll have to get to know the men when we're in the field."

"We're headed back to the front, sir?"

"Yep, Top, I've received a warning order. We're going to be moving … well, most of the damned First Army … is moving about sixty miles north."

"A new assault, sir?"

"Yeah. Keep it on the QT for now. Platoon commanders and NCOs will get a complete read-in soon. Meanwhile, what shape are we in?"

"Well, sir, the company came out of that fight in pretty fair condition. Platoon strength is supposed to be 58 men and right now on average we're at about 40. I'm told a dozen lightly wounded will be back soon and battalion called to say we're to receive 15 replacements."

"Damn, that's all? Okay Max, be sure you ride herd on the medical people. We don't want any of our recovered wounded malingering in hospitals. They're veterans and we need all the veterans we can get. Now, the replacements? Are they green kids?"

"I'd say it's likely, sir."

He sighed. "Yeah well, that's war, ain't it? You're always short on everything but enemy."

"Oh, sir, we do have some good news there. Our gear is almost complete. We even got a full issue of greatcoats which I've got the feeling we're going to need."

"Good! Now what about training for the green kids?"

"Sir, I'll want you to meet Sergeant Adamczak. He's a Princeton man, a damn good Chauchat gunner, and he's been in charge of training for … hell, sir, I can't remember … but he's very good at it. And I think if the opportunity arises he'd make an excellent commissioned officer."

"Have him report to me. I want to meet him first chance we get. And if he's that good, I have a present for him. I brought a new weapon that's just trickling into France now -- the Browning Automatic Rifle. It serves either as a rifle or machine gun. A twenty-round mag -- a box magazine, not wide open to dirt and crap like that damned Chauchat.

"And Max, they designed the BAR specifically for .30-06 ammo. It's *not* made of bicycle tubing and I hear it almost never jams.

"How many did you bring, sir?"

"I could only scrounge two."

"Well, okay, sir. I'd like to fire one before Adamczak gets it and I recommend the second one to go to Sergeant Zimmer."

# # #

"Gentlemen, I won't mince words. This attack is going to be tough."

Major Crain, the battalion operations officer, tacked up a large map. It showed the center of the Western Front with a 150-mile semicircular bulge. The bulge enclosed Bosche-occupied territory – basically the gains of the Germans' spring offensives.

"The allies' goal is to drive the Bosche out of that territory. And from here on," he said, "the strategy is to attack and keep attacking here one day, there the next and so on everywhere into that semicircle.

"The British will attack up here …" he pointed to the northwest rim of the circle. Then, pointing to the west margins of the circle. "The French here.

"And down here to the south is our piece of the pie. We're attacking for the first time as an all-American force. In fact, it's three whole corps now officially the American First Army.

"The base of our pie slice is roughly twenty miles wide. The pointed tip of the slice, thirty miles to the north, is Sedan, a French city under Bosche control since August 1914.

"In some ways," the major said, "our mission is just the same as our attack toward Soissons. We need to cut the north-south railways and roads that supply every Fritz with every bullet he fires and every loaf of black bread that feeds him. Cut that line and he has no choice but to evacuate France."

He took a breath.

"So," Lieutenant Graham said, "what makes it so tough?"

"Right," Lieutenant Carney said, "other than the fact that German engineers have had three solid years to fortify the area."

"Yes," Major Crain said, "there's that. And two other factors also intervene. First off, we'll be attacking up a valley dominated on the west by the Argonne Forest and on the right by the bluffs along the Meuse river.

"The forest and the Meuse lie parallel to each other, so our forces will be under artillery observation …"

"And fire," Lieutenant Rogers said.

"Yes, from both sides," Major Crain added.

"And it won't help that the valley itself looks a lot like the hills in Pennsylvania or West Virginia. Lots of steep slopes, deep ravines, false crests, narrow gullies and granite cliffs … great terrain for defenders, very tough to attack."

"Looks like a damned shooting gallery," Lieutenant Carney said.

Lieutenant Schreiber chimed in, "I think we're headed up the Valley of Death. How does it go? 'Ours not to reason why; ours but to do and …'"

Captain Blackmun snapped an icy, "At ease, lieutenant! Let's permit the major to complete his briefing." The major nodded his thanks to the captain.

"We're trying some deception moves to divert their attention elsewhere. And what I hadn't mentioned so far is that the French Fourth Army under our favorite, General Gouraud, will attack into the Argonne from the west. Should keep the Bosche in the woods at least somewhat occupied.

"And we won't be alone," the major added. "In fact, our operation will be but one segment of a step-by-step assault by the allies. The plan is to wear Fritz down by forcing him to constantly switch forces from one front to another."

He wrapped up claiming we'd have the benefit of surprise.

"Gentlemen, we're moving hundreds of thousands of troops – plus all of their artillery – and we're doing it by night. The Bosche command certainly knows something's up, but they won't know where we'll strike because their fliers won't see our movements."

# # #

"Good Lord, bless us," Adamczak said as we walked back to our tents. "Move us at night on these gawdawful roads?"

"Yeah," I said. "Just one division's artillery pieces alone takes up about ten miles of road. And I know it takes damned near a thousand trucks to move the troops of one measly division."

It hit me I might be depressing one of our best leaders.

"But at least," I said, "the French will prrovide most of the artillery. Even better, they're the ones who'll transport us and they've had a hell of a lot of experience at it."

Chapter 49

On The Move – September 1918

"Koddam, dis is crazy! Now I know how dat Taylor woman felt."

"Abelyan, you crazy Armenian," I said, "what in the hell are you nattering about?"

"When we hit beeg, beeg chuckholes, my teeths clicks togedder. I feel like dat lady what went over big waterfall. Niagra, you know? Only *she* lived. I don't tink we will."

Just then our camion slammed into another huge bump, producing a chorus of angry yells.

"Eddie, switch that bayonet scabbard out of my ribs afore I throw you out of this truck!"

"Blow it out your ass, Sam! I can't move and I ain't got no room to move nothin'."

As the driver ground the gears to pull us out of the dip, I had to agree. He had no room to move.

Nobody did.

The Frog transport people literally crammed us into these little trucks.

We were wedged together on benches, rifles held betwixt our knees, backpacks keeping us from resting our spines against the bench backs. Gas masks, canteens, pistols, binocular cases, and cartridge pouches smothered arm movement.

We even were carrying one of those 80-pound machinegun tripods.

Yet more men were huddled knees to backs on the truck floor.

It was a jarring slam-bang hour since one of the Frogs, a genial giant, shouted, "Okay, American friends! *Dépêchez-vous, Teddies! Dans les Camions!"* as he practically tossed us into the truck.

"What's 'daypeeshay'? What the hell's he saying?"

"You stupid palooka, he's telling you to hurry up and get into the damned truck. What do you think he's saying?"

"Well, it looks pretty crowded!"

"It is. So git in anyway and quit bitching!"

As a final insult, once we piled aboard cramming shoulder to shoulder, the giant tossed three featherweights among us.

Even though the last three men were light, they still were a burden, all being laden with the same hard, pointed gear.

All of us, of course, were swaddled in our new thick greatcoats so that it literally was impossible to do more than wiggle your fingers or turn your head.

"Jesus, my rifle bolt handle's digging into my leg!"

"Live, with it, trooper! We only got another three or four hours of this!"

"Or maybe five."

The guys bitched constantly and I didn't blame them. The other convoys of supplies and artillery had so deeply rutted the roads, that the bone-rattling bumps made it impossible to even doze.

Somebody said. "Jesus, Mary and Joseph! The goddamned generals want us to fight the Bosche after taking this ride through hell?"

# # #

Jesus, Mary and Joseph must have heard that young soldier's prayer because I Corps held us in reserve for the first two days of the attack.

Artillery was firing from behind us, shells ripping the air overhead then plunging into the Argonne forest.

We could see the crest of those wooded hills, but little of the artillery strikes. The forest seemed to absorb high explosives like a giant green sponge.

Trying to help new men relax, I asked a tough-looking Iowa farm boy, "How you doing Willard?"

He swallowed. "Well, we ain't fighting but we sure as hell can tell that somebody is."

"Yep, not our turn yet" I said. "The 28th Division is charging into those woods, cutting a path for us."

"Yes," Lieutenant Graham said. "And going right beside them is the 35th, fresh from the States. They haven't been off the boat more than two weeks or had any time in action at all. And I've got a cousin who's with them."

"Damn," I thought. "Good luck to him."

At our distance we could hear a faint but growing rattle, as if a giant were snapping a million sticks – mass rifle and machinegun fire.

The U.S. First Army was attacking and the Bosche were fighting back for all they were worth.

Chapter 50

Finding The Front – October 1, 1918

"Something's wrong," I said.

Captain Blackmun nodded bitterly. "I'm afraid you're right, Max."

Orders from Chaumont moved and deployed First Division two more times in four days, huge undertakings that shifted and exhausted twenty-two thousand men. First they crammed us like sardines into camions and took us east into V Corps and then turned us west back into I Corps.

To make things worse, steady cold rain set in, often with sleet tinking on our helmets. The rain beaded up on our greatcoats, but over time the moisture penetrated everywhere and chilled everything.

"What bothers me," the skipper said, "is that all this racing around – plus willy-nilly switching division and corps boundaries -- has snarled up our supply trains. Supplies aren't reaching us and when they send us to attack, the men might have only their basic ammo load."

"Maybe I ought to check in with battalion …"

"Shit, Max, I already did. I talked with Major Creek and they and regiment are as bamboozled as us. They've been burning up the phone lines to Chaumont. The problem seems to be that Blackjack is trying to run both the whole damned theater *and* First Army. We're talking about more than a million American troops."

"Sir, I'm sure you're right," I said. "But there's something else on my mind. I've been talking to the wounded that they're bringing back from the 35th. Scads of them.

"They all claim those hills are murder. They said they advanced and suddenly were getting attacked from behind."

"Were you talking with some new shavetail?"

"Nossir!"

# # #

When I visited the aid station, I actually did see one shavetail, but he wasn't speaking. He probably never would.

In the litter beside him was an old sergeant, a guy named Morton. I knew him from Mexico days. He was biting his lower lip because of pain, but he spoke clearly and bitterly.

"Watch out when you go up there," he told me. "The ground is a bitch. It's got all kinds of overlapping ridges with big gullies that break up any advance. It's kind of like those foothills we saw in Chihuahua, you know, but these ones got some pretty thick woods.

"Anyhow, you start advancing, company in line, you know. But pretty soon you're climbing a slope or going 'round a knoll. And the squad beside you – or the squad that *was* beside you – heads into a gully or up the far side of a spur. Before you know it most of your squads is out of touch with each other and headquarters don't know shit.

"That's when the Huns strike. You don't see them. Just flash and smoke of their weapons and a lotta green tracers, but by then half your squad is down. You tell the boys to fire back, but most of 'em just stand there lookin' around with their mouths open, until they get hit."

As we talked the red stains on his muddy bandages slowly spread. Then he passed out and I headed back to Company B.

# # #

"Cap'n, he told me the hills ahead of us force movement onto diverging tracks, so there's a lot of confusion about where the front is. Flanks are wide open. Nobody knows what's happening even a hundred yards away.

"Sir, 35th Division troops are green as grass. They haven't learned to read the ground or got the knack of keeping in touch or making sense about what they hear going on next door. Looks like some of them by-passed Bosche gun pits and then got a Maxim hosing from behind."

"I see," the captain nodded. "And then they started taking grenades and rifle fire from the front. It's a wonder anyone got back alive."

He got the platoon commanders and NCOs together.

"Men, this is going to be a corporal's fight. The squads will conduct this battle because it'll be impossible for me or the other officers to exercise very much control. As always, we'll depend on runners, but in this terrain they may not make it through.

"If you haven't done this already, find your squads' deer hunters. Send them ahead to scout. We've got to know the ground and where the Huns are. Then we attack, and not before.

"We'll need all the grenades the men can carry," he added.

"Sorry sir," Lieutenant Rogers said, "but we've got no damned grenades and we have no more than the ready load for our mortars. Seems like regimental supply hasn't caught up with us yet."

"Why am I not surprised?" the captain said. "But we've got no choice. First Division is ordered to relieve the 35th tonight so our whole division will move up there.

"Where exactly, sir?"

"We're to advance north paralleling the base of the Argonne forest. The 28th Division will be on our left in the forest proper and 91st Division will be on our right.

"Our orders are to deploy along a front extending from Serieux to Chaudron. The map isn't real clear about where that front is or our place in it. So this afternoon, Max, I want you with battalion's operations officer -- you remember Major Crain -- to see where they want us to deploy."

"Hoo, boy," I said.

"Keep your head down, Max."

"You bet, sir."

# # #

The major had a lieutenant and four riflemen with him.

"We're headed for HQ of the 65th Infantry," he said. "All we'll do is check their dispositions and then stand by 'til after sundown when our troops come to replace them.

Approaching 65th headquarters ignited a volcano. A shrill shriek opened the eruption. As an old hand, I sensed the shell headed straight toward us. I screamed "Down!" and scuttled into a muddy groove alongside our road. The first explosion was every bit as shocking as a surprise body block.

It just got worse. A giant – an enormous, evil, shrieking, drooling, maddened, red-eyed giant – stamped his huge jackboots on me again and again and again. The blasts pushed spikes through my chest. Needles ricocheted inside my skull.

More shrieks and thunderclaps made me cower, digging fingers and pressing my face into the mud. The next blasts were worse and seemed closer. The pain worsened. "My God, please make them let up! Please! *Please! God I beg you, make it stop!"*

It took far too long to stop.

Once it stopped, I waited to arise. A perfect rhythmic noise, kind of a pulse – "Uh. Uh. Uh. Uh." – demanded that I get up. Getting to hands and knees was almost impossible because I virtually had to peel myself out of the sucking mud.

Standing was hard. My balance seemed shot, forcing me to take baby steps.

The lieutenant looked to have absorbed the strike of one of those 77 mm Bosche shells.

The "Uh. Uh. Uh." came from the major, a glistening red canyon stretching diagonally across his back. I staggered toward him but he became silent. His body subsided.

Three riflemen quietly arose, wiping mud from their weapons.

"What now, sarge?"

I barely heard his voice.

"We'd best continue on to the 35th."

Chapter 51

Facing the Fire – October 1918

Andy splashed down beside me in my shell hole. "Well, Max, looks like we're all done with trench warfare."

"So what is it now, Andy, shell hole warfare?"

"Naaaa, I don't think so," he said. "Seems to me more like pudding warfare – fighting knee-deep in chocolate pudding."

I was in no mood to joke. "Maybe it looks like chocolate," I said, giving a futile swipe at the slop on my rifle's action. "Smells more like shit."

"Well, yeah."

We peered through the rain at the crest of the cratered ridge before us. Shattered tree trunks jutted from the ridge crest. They looked like so many graveyard headstones. But the Germans up there were very lively.

The banshee shriek of incoming artillery made us both flatten ourselves into the mud of our hole. "Oh, God." Andy said. "Sounds to me like a nine …"

The earth rocked and heaved to an enormous, shattering blast. Shrapnel slapped into the mud around us. Then mud clots thrown aloft by the explosive pattered down onto us.

"…a nine-incher," Andy continued. "It's like some giant trying to stamp a pair of ants with both boots."

Terror had me shivering. "L-l-l-look on the bright side. At least the Huns are creating more shell holes for us."

"Can it, Max! My God, why the hell does headquarters keep us out here in this fucking shooting gallery? *Why?* Bosche artillery's blasting us from them Argonne woods to the left and from the right, from the bluffs along the Meuse."

"Tell me something I don't know."

"Max, we're just not doing any good here in between the Hun positions except maybe making them waste ammo on us. Do the generals actually *want* the Huns to destroy us?"

I dodged the subject. I turned to him. "Say, Andy, d'you recall that Independence Day parade in Chicago back in '09?"

"Yeah," he gave me a grimace of a grin, "and that recruiter with all his bullshit? And speaking of bullshit, just why the hell are you talking about this?"

"To take my mind off this shelling."

"Oh. Okay, I'll play along. So, do you suppose if we'd stayed at the Yard instead of enlisting in this outfit, we might be running Armour or Swift by now?"

"Oh, I doubt it, Andy. More likely we'd just be a couple of foremen in that slaughterhouse."

The banshee scream rose again, closer this time, becoming a train's roar. *"Oh no! Oh no! Oh no! Get flat!"*

The big shell must have exploded within yards of our hole. The earth slammed up against us, feeling it had caved in my ribs. The pressure from the blast stunned us both. Then a fountain of mud collapsed upon us like a filthy bedspread.

Andy recovered first. "Just like we are now," he said.

"What?"

"Right now we're no better than a couple of foremen in a slaughterhouse."

I nodded. "Yep, Andy. But right now I just want to be thinking on how smart that parade company looked. Remember? Spotless khakis. Razor creases. Perfect straight brims on those old campaign hats. Boots all shined. Officers carrying swords."

He said, "It was a full company, wasn't it? About 200 men."

I gave a sour laugh. "You had to mention that. Well, now my friend, last I heard we're down to 83 men – hardly two platoons."

I took a deep breath. "And what a bunch of ragpickers B Company looks right now."

Here it came again. A scream dropping to a roar. *"My God! My God! My God!"*

God had mercy on us. The huge shell didn't land so close. Neither did two more blasts. Then the shelling seemed to peter off. Andy and I split up to tour the line of holes that B Company occupied.

"Crockett, how's it going?"

"Well, not so hot, Sarge. One of them big shells landed smack inside the hole next to ours. Left me damn near deef. And Lieutenant Graham was in there, so I'd say that the Bosche artillery has put you in command."

That was news I didn't need. "You sure?"

"Look for yourself, Top. Nothing left over there but a hole."

"Okay, Davie, how about you take off for headquarters? Let 'em know to send us a new officer. Tell 'em we're probably down to 80 effectives."

He looked me in the eye. "I might not come back."

"Well, don't let MPs catch you. They'd throw you in the stockade."

He snorted. "Better than being up here."

After he took off, I dodged along the left of our line ducking machinegun bursts. Shrapnel had virtually torn VanderStelt in two and badly injured three other men.

Back at our little headquarters crater, Andy said, "Bad news. Two more dead and five wounded, two seriously.

"Okay, and three bad injuries on the left." I said. "Organize stretcher bearers to take the wounded back after dark."

"Got it, Max."

"And as far as I'm concerned, once there you all can catch a nap once. Then see if they have any grenades."

"Ammo, too," he said. "The boys are running short."

Chapter 52

Into the Jaws – October 1918

In five minutes I'd blow my whistle and the remnants of Company B would arise from the mud to assault the ridge.

"The boys are ready," Andy said.

"I'm not."

I was still trying to get my head around Crockett's arrival at our shell hole just before dawn. "Sir," he said, "I've got some news."

"Knock off the 'sir', Crockett. I'm your first sergeant."

Gloating, he said, "Not no more, sir. Colonel Creek promoted you to first lieutenant. Said you was to continue commanding B Company. And it's long overdue, he claimed."

Andy held out his hand, "Congratulations, Max."

"Congratulations my ass! I didn't really need this right now. I take it Creek now is the lieutenant colonel commanding."

"Yessir," Crockett said, "being's how *his* boss took over as regimental CO. He's a bird colonel now."

I stewed about my promotion until a fitful barrage began exploding along the crest of the ridge. "About time," Andy said. "I hope for once the artillery gives us more than ten minutes."

"But what really scares me," he joked, "is that you're in command again."

"Well, so what? You're acting exec. That's just as scary. I can recommend that the old man promote you to lieutenant."

"No thanks, sir. I'd just as soon stay a sergeant. Besides, there ain't much company left to be exec of. The Bosche have just about done us in."

"No," I snapped. "Thank the high command. A fella can hardly walk through this fudge, let alone run. We've been catching fire from both sides for more than a week. And still no grenades! Damn little food and we have to drink water out of these shell holes!

"But, oh boy, those fat swells at Division HQ with their champagne and steak want this droopy-assed group to charge the Huns again. And you know why?"

"Why?"

"When the stretcher-bearers hauled Schreiber away, he gave me his folded-up copy of a First Army circular. It seems that Blackjack wants us Yanks to keep piling headlong into the Bosche to preserve our offensive spirit."

"You're shitting me."

"I am not. And now, Andy, I see by my watch it's time for me to blow my little whistle."

Another deep breath to quell my fear.

"Get ready, Andy, and keep your head down."

He grinned, gave me a salute, and said, "Aye, aye, sir."

I pulled the nickel-plated police whistle from my breast pocket and blew it so hard my ears popped. Andy and I clambered from our shell hole, waved our arms toward the ridge and began moving up the slope.

The men, all looking like tar babies, arose yelling on both sides of us.

Despite our barrage, the crest of the ridge began flickering with gun flashes, turning the air around us alive with vicious hums.

The men knew the drill, though. We all advanced, then flopped into shell holes – fair cover for rifle and machinegun fire. We began careful aimed fire. Then, in ones and twos, we'd pop out of concealment, race forward and dash and splash into the next hole.

"Jesus this water's cold!"

"Stop bitching," Andy said through quivering lips. "It may be freezing, but beats a bullet in the face."

"Pardon me for bitching," I said, as I aimed and fired my Springfield. While cranking the bolt, I caught sight of Adamzcak firing short bursts with his BAR.

Then, very faintly, I hear the *thonk*.

"Hell! Mortars on the way."

Andy grinned at me as he raised up to fire. "Max, please stay low, will you? I don't want to be in command of this lash-up."

Bullets whipped the rim of our shell hole to a brown mist. The slugs hurled Andy onto his back. Blood spurted from his mouth and neck.

I frantically splashed to him, clapping a field dressing against his neck. I cradled him in my arms. By now, daily slaughter inured me to death, even my own likely death. But not Andy's, for God's sake. Anybody but Andy, my chum since childhood.

He coughed, turned his eyes to me and gurgled through his blood, "Guess I'm hit pretty bad, Max."

"Andy, you stupid bastard! For Christ's sake, why didn't you stay low and hold fire? You shouldn't have … awwww, *God!*"

He gurgled again, "Ain't dying am I?"

He coughed and his body shrank as his life left. I seemed to feel a tiny gust, the soul impatiently elbowing past me. Briefly I sensed him eagerly joining ten thousand other spirits soaring up and away from this stench, freed of the filth, already reveling in quiet and peace.

Part of me died with Andy. But only part. I wasn't freed yet.

In savage jealousy I screamed, "Damn you, Andy!" and plunged my hands into the muck to hide his blood.

Then there was nothing to do but get up and go kill those murderers at the crest of the ridge.

# # #

I recall advancing in a daze.

Mortars landed here and there, but I never took cover. I didn't care if they killed me.

I recall walking and aiming, my left side toward the Bosche, faintly hoping I was thin enough their shots wouldn't hit me.

Somehow none did. Probably that was thanks to BAR fire from Adamczak and Zimmer and the other gunners with their Chauchats. Or maybe our so-called offensive spirit actually cowed the Huns.

I kept yelling, "Surrender you bastards! Drop your guns. Hands up!" I chanted it, over and over, the way some of those Catholic kids say their beads. Except I didn't murmur. I bellowed loud as I could, all the time cranking the bolt, putting my sights on coal scuttle helmets and pulling the trigger. I think I nailed maybe six of those bastards.

Shooting too, the rest of the company advanced in line with me. It was exactly the way we weren't supposed to assault because they'd slaughter us.

As we got close, some Huns took off to their rear. Others put their hands up. We piled down into their trench, tearing into the armed ones with butts and bayonets.

Crockett found two crates of stick grenades and handed them out. The boys yanked the strings from the handles and hurled the grenades as far as they could along the Huns' communication trenches.

After an advance on our part, the Bosche always mortared us and then counterattacked. This day they didn't. Zimmer helped me wrench around one of the Bosche Maxims to point north. I fired it, sending green tracers toward their mortar crews. Empty casings showering into a glittering brass pile.

Meanwhile, an attack by the 28th Division on our left seemed to start a Bosche panic.

So we were able to hold our ridge.

I promoted Adamczak to first sergeant and appointed him as my executive officer. I'd no idea if I had the right to promote anybody to anything but I was so sick at heart I didn't care.

"Bill, the first thing you need to do," I said, "is find someone to replace you as BAR gunner."

He started to reply, but I just overrode him. "Next, call roll and get the butcher bill to me."

He reported back later. "Well, sir, that assault cost us a dozen killed and thirty-two wounded. Eight of the wounded are are pretty seriously hurt."

It made me feel like more of a murderer than the enemy. My assault damned near wiped us out. I had to inform battalion that Company B was down to 41 effectives.

They pulled us from the line.

Chapter 53

An End In Sight – October '18

Lieutenant Colonel Creek handed me my silver bars. "Congratulation, Max. I only hope you don't have to remain in grade a lieutenant as long as I had to."

I barely grinned at his joke. With my 10-year buddy buried and A Company sliced to platoon size, I felt utterly desolate.

Seeing my mood, the colonel said, "You'll be as pleased to learn that First Army will pause for a few days. General Pershing turned First Army over to General Liggett and he's getting things organized. God knows we need it."

"I know, sir. Grenades, mortar ammo, food, water – none of it getting to us."

"Right! Nor to much of anybody else, either" he said. "I know your casualties. And Company B isn't alone. Third Battalion is down to just about two hundred men."

I just shook my head.

"The rear areas were in a sheer tangle," he said. "Nothing was getting through to anybody.

"Well, two days ago Liggett got the engineers to graveling and corduroying roads so now supplies are moving. He also clarified unit boundaries. From now on his staff – and *only* his staff -- will change them. No more muddling by the map and crayon jockeys at Chaumont.

"Meanwhile," he added, "this battalion is due to get a good-sized draft of replacements."

"Sir, how about some more BARs?"

"None available until spring," the colonel said. "Too bad. It's a fine weapon. But, here's great news. Even better than a promotion."

"What's that, sir?"

He held up *Stars and Stripes* to show me a splashy banner headline. "Last week the British broke through in Mesopotamia and the Turks are quitting the war!"

The day suddenly brightened. "Hot damn," I said. "The end actually may be in sight? Didn't I hear Bulgaria deserted the Kaiser? Hell, some of us actually might survive this thing."

# # #

When I got back to the company, some of the boys were making gobbling noises. News about Turkey had spread.

But we also heard it still was a bloody grind up on the line. Despite what happened to their allies, Germans were fighting with every bit of their old determination, skill and stubbornness.

Meanwhile, A Company received 100 replacements. They were just off the boat and excited to take on the Bosche.

"Bill, what do you think of them so far?"

"God help us," Adamczak said. "They're bubbling over with enthusiasm as if they're all suited up for Saturday's big game against Harvard or something. But they aren't as fit as the old gang and, from what I've seen, their marksmanship isn't as good."

"So God help *them*," I said. "We've got to go back into the line in three days. No time to really train them. So, Bill, you've just got to spread them into the three platoons."

"Three?"

"Yeah, we haven't the manpower for four.

"First, have a talk with the old hands. We can't expect them to lead these kids by the hand. But at least they can tell them to copy the veterans' actions – and never to hesitate to dive flat into the mud."

"Very good, sir," he said.

So, a company of 152 Yanks marched back north into the Valley of Death.

This time it was an eight-mile hike. First Army had gained a fair amount of ground. That also included the capture of a towering hill from which the Huns had bedeviled us since the the attack began.

As we drew nearer, combat noises grew louder and the new troops' high spirits toned down. When we reached our front, I turned to Guardino. "Seems like fireworks sober these young devils."

"Well, sir, that's probably part of it," he said.

"But the main thing was seeing swelled-up American bodies crawling with flies. It shows them what's what. You know what I mean?"

"Harry, I know exactly what you mean. I just hope they pay attention to the old hands."

"Gotta go, sir. Here's that knoll you assigned us boys in Third Platoon."

"Keep your head down, Harry."

"You know it, sir."

He trotted to his platoon. One of his corporals was yelling. "Now if you bastards wanna live, keep your spread. You may want to be right next to your buddy, but that gits you both killed."

Guardino patted his shoulder. "That's right! And when we take fire, stay low, stay apart and shoot back!

"Now, first squad stays here in reserve. Second and third, start circling this little hill, second left, third to the right . . ."

# # #

It was a noisy day. Adamczak had to take over First Platoon when DeVries was killed. I filled in for Zimmerman when a shell landed too close and knocked him cold.

We couldn't capture the crest of the ridge. It lay atop a long, gullied slope with no cover other than stunted bushes. But thanks to our scouts and the way we copied Guardino – one squad watching two squads' backs – we discovered and cleared some cunningly concealed Bosche machineguns positions. We settled in for the night in just those positions and a chain of shell holes.

At dusk a runner came back to me. "Lieutenant, sir, Sergeant Guardino reports his line is pretty secure. He said to tell you he circled the wagons and can fire in all directions except on the right where he's in touch with First Platoon. Wants more grenades. And he's got two scouts out checking things. We lost nine people today, sir.

"Just one other bad thing, sir."

"What's that?"

"Well, these Hun positions is filled with lice. And the Huns shit in there, too. It stinks somethin' fierce."

"Beats being dead, though, don't it?"

"Well, yessir."

At dark, our quartermaster loomed out of the rain bringing a full load of ammo, grenades and water. So we were as ready as we could be when the mortars coughed and the shells started crashing among us. It was a sure and certain sign the Bosche would attack.

I yelled, "Keep an eye skinned downhill, too. The Huns like to come at you where you least expect them."

That's exactly what they did. During the night they harassed us off and on with machineguns at the crest while dropping mortar rounds among us. But then about 0400 -- when the desire to sleep is worst – it all stopped.

Adamczak yelled, "Stay alert! It's too quiet."

The Fritzes came boiling up the slope behind us, firing those little submachine guns. We met them with fire and steel.

"Thank God," I muttered as I hurled my fifth grenade down the slope. It exploded practically at the knees of three Huns coming toward us. Grenades, theirs and ours, were exploding all up and down our slope.

At dawn, everyone looked gray, staring into the distance.

I hated it, but I had my orders.

"Let's go! We've still got to take this Goddamned ridge."

Chapter 54

The Victory – November '18

They say our attacks between the Argonne Forest and the bluffs of the Meuse River broke the German Army's back. Others say the price Yanks paid in that hell-hole – almost 30,000 killed in action – broke the will of Ludendorff, Hindenberg and the Kaiser.

All I know for sure is that once atop our ridge, I collapsed. Adamczak took command, ordering me and a dozen other men evacuated. Shrapnel and bullets wounded eight of them. Spanish Influenza flattened the other five.

Since then, I've read that the 1918-1919 flu pandemic killed more Frogs, Brits, Yanks and Huns than high explosives, bullets and lousy generals.

I'd have died if I hadn't almost killed some orderly. The twit tried to keep me lying on a cot. I slammed him aside, barely managed to get up and found a chair.

Seated backwards, arms resting on the chair back and head resting on my arms, I could breathe again. I dozed between racking coughs that brought up the gray-green gluey phlegm which drowned so many men lying on cots.

Once able to gasp out five consecutive words, I tried to raise hell. "Killing these men! Unheated tent in October? Oh, November now? One blanket apiece? They're freezing, damn you! Where're the docs?"

Riverss of wounded had overwhelmed surgeons and nurses. At that point, flu victims were on their own.

Later, Division drove me and several other half-recovered officers to a rest home outside Paris. With warmth and decent food, I recovered fairly quickly. At lunch on November 11 we drank more

than was wise, celebrating the armistice that ended the killing …
though not the dying.

Six days later, I was enroute to the 16th Infantry back at its
first French home, Gondrecourt. Beyond shaking hands with
Colonel Creek, Lieutenant Adamczak and Sergeants Guardino and
Crockett, it was a subdued reunion. Very few old hands remained. I
kept half-expecting to see Andy.

We got very busy receiving and training new recruits for our
invasion of Germany.

"Under the armistice terms," Colonel Creek explained,
"we're part of the Army of Occupation. We'll march to Coblenz to
maintain a bridgehead there. So get our new people trained! Train
them hard! We assume the Huns won't resist, but if they do, we
want the troops prepared."

Days later Adamczak repored, "They're not resisting. Our
patrols ran into lots of Fritz companies waiting their turn to march to
their home towns. At first it was very stiff. It's damned eerie to meet
a Fritz loaded with ammo pouches and carrying his Mauser.

"But our kids broke the ice – the kids just off the boat, I
mean. They never saw combat and almost seemed to admire Huns.
They started trading cigarettes for German belts, decoration ribbons
and cap badges…that kind of thing. Lugers were selling at a
premium.

"The Bosche are so starved for food and good tobacco,
they're happy to trade. Even the junior officers. They hear that
Sparticists and red revolutionaries back home strip insignia from
officers' uniforms."

Late in November, the 16th Infantry – eighty percent new
faces – led the 200-mile march from Gondrecourt to Coblenz.

The French cheered us and waved goodbye. The Belgians
cheered us and waved as we passed through. The German welcome
was cold as the weather -- blinds drawn, people scurrying indoors.

Snow and ice made it a hard trek, but on December 17, we
entered Coblenz marching in step. Coblenz (nowadays spelled with
a K) is an impressive city where the Moselle River joins the Rhine.

A huge bluff topped with an enormous fortress frowns down on the community.

The troops were excited and wanted to explore, but we kept drilling them.

At first, the citizens were almost cringing and wouldn't meet our eyes. When they realized we weren't there to rape and pillage, they relaxed and eventually some of them became friendly.

"I'm billeted with a teacher and his family," Adamczak said. "When I came to the front door he scowled. His frau threw her apron over her face and raced to the kitchen. The two little sons stood in the door of my bedroom as I unpacked my duffle but disappeared when Dad snapped, 'Raus!'

"It shocked him when I spoke German. Then he tried his English on me and asked that I help his sons with *their* English. Then he really shocked his frau by inviting me to dinner."

I was billeted with an aged couple and their son, a former German Army captain who had lost his right arm in combat. They were reserved. He was bitter, but not about the arm.

"The allies blame German for everything," he said. "They still blockade our ports so that people in the north are starving. And our delegation at the Versailles Treaty talks are imprisoned behind barbed wire. This is insane!"

He said certain domestic political factions already were starting to blame bankers, industrialists and Jews for Germany's defeat.

"I tell you, Lieutenant Coleman, I fear your children and my children will fight this war again."

I nodded. "I sincerely hope not," I said. "One war like this is enough."

"Enough for the world, I agree," he said. "But more will come, I fear."

I should have paid more attention, but didn't. Something else, something bright, was on my mind.

I had just read three letters from Maria Gonzalez.

She mailed the letters last year but their envelopes were covered with many scribbled Post Office instructions about locating one "Sergeant Colman" among the two million Yanks with the US Army in Europe.

Her first letter thanked me and my friends – most of them dead now -- for her wonderful *quinceanera.*

The others were more personal, asking about after my health and promising many prayers for my safety. "I also send many kisses," she wrote.

I hear that the 16th Infantry, the first to arrive will be the first to leave – that we'll ship home this coming summer.

When we arrive in the states, I'll ask for leave.

 I think I'll catch the train to El Paso.

About The Author

J. Scott Payne began his writing career as a cub reporter with the *Kansas City Star*. He served with the Army in Korea, Vietnam and – worst of all – Washington, D.C. Subsequently he worked as a reporter and editor for several midwestern newspapers and magazines. He and Jane retired to a small college town in west Michigan where they enjoy the woods, the birds and the battles – or maybe the games – taking place between Burt, their big black cat, and Bailey, their white terrier.

www.ingramcontent.com/pod-product-compliance
Lightning Source LLC
Chambersburg PA
CBHW071236250626
47163CB00001B/208